Al[illegible]per Lin

The Patisserie Mysteries
Macaron Murder: Book 1
Éclair Murder: Book 2
Baguette Murder: Book 3
Crêpe Murder: Book 4
Croissant Murder: Book 5
Crème Brûlée Murder: Book 6
Madeleine Murder: Book 7

The Emma Wild Mysteries
4-Book Holiday Series
Killer Christmas: Book 1
New Year's Slay: Book 2
Death of a Snowman: Book 3
Valentine's Victim: Book 4

The Wonder Cats Mysteries
A Hiss-tory of Magic: Book 1

www.HarperLin.com

Madeleine Murder

A Patisserie Mystery
Book #7

by Harper Lin

This is a work of fiction. Names, characters, organizations, places, events, and incidents are either products of the author's imagination or are used fictitiously. Some street names and locations in Paris are real, and others are fictitious.

ISBN-13: 978-0993949500

ISBN-10: 0993949509

Contents

Recipes

Chapter 1

Clémence Damour didn't know when she fell asleep on Arthur's shoulder in the taxi. After three hours on a train that took them from Amsterdam Central Station to Gare du Nord Station in Paris, she had been exhausted. The slow journey from the station to her apartment in the 16th had a lulling effect on her. All the Parisians seem to be returning to Paris from their summer vacations at the same time.

When the taxi lurched to a stop, her eyes flew open, and she looked around in a daze.

"Enjoyed your nap?" Arthur shot her a cute smile. A lock of his chestnut brown hair fell over one eye. As sleepy as she felt, she couldn't help but reach a hand up and brush the lock from his face in a sweet gesture.

"Looks like we're back in Paris," she said wryly.

It was car-to-car gridlock. August was almost over, and the city was back to being business as usual.

Their taxi driver honked, joining in on the melody of car honks. "*Merde!*" he exclaimed, shaking his head. *"C'est incroyable."* He said it as if he'd never been stuck in traffic before in his life.

"The stresses of modern living," Arthur mused. "It would probably be faster if we walked home."

"We could if we didn't have our luggage," Clémence said with a voice still groggy with sleep.

Her whole body was feeling the effects of bicycling around the Netherlands for the last seven days. It wasn't fair–since the Dutch begin cycling as soon as they learned to walk, they have had a whole lifetime to develop thighs of steel. Not only were Clémence's legs sore, but her butt hurt, and even her arms and shoulders were recovering from gripping her handlebars for dear life while cycling in central Amsterdam.

The taxi started moving again at a snail's pace. At least they were right along the Seine, and Clémence could enjoy the view of the famous river. The car inched up the street like a tortoise until they reached Pont des Alexandre III. There were thirty-seven bridges across the Seine, and Pont Alexandre III was her favorite. She wasn't alone in that sentiment. It was by far the most extravagant, with ornate Art Nouveau lamps and massive sculptures of cherubs and winged horses guarding each end. At night, when all the bridges were lit up, it was such a pretty scene. The bridge was a frequent backdrop in films and ad campaigns.

"What's going on up there?" Clémence poked her head out the window.

A crowd had gathered at the base of the bridge. She strained her neck and saw the ambulance truck and three police cars parked along the sidewalk.

"They're probably filming something," the gruff taxi driver said. "It's been that way for weeks now, streets randomly being closed around the city for those Hollywood films." He let out a long, exasperated sigh.

"I don't think it's a movie shoot, *monsieur*," Clémence said.

There were no cameras or lighting equipment as far as she could see. Clémence had passed by plenty of television and film productions in Paris, especially since she lived and worked near Trocadéro, the area with the best view of the Eiffel Tower. She'd also seen crews filming in cafés, bookstores, and along the Seine. Once she saw Audrey Tautou in the Tuileries Gardens, filming a scene for a romantic comedy.

"Maybe there's been an accident," Arthur said.

The cab lurched closer to the scene, but it stalled again.

"Maybe." Clémence was fully awake now. Curiosity was brimming inside her. Was it another murder? Less than an hour back in Paris and she was already encountering another murder? *C'est impossible.*

"Are you okay?" Arthur examined her.

"Fine. Why?"

"You look a bit too anxious." He smiled wryly.

"It's because I think you're right. I bet there's been an accident of some sort. But I'm not going to check it out."

She sat on her hands, as if that would contain her curiosity. After their murder-free vacation, did she want to get herself involved in yet another gruesome murder case?

She bet Inspector Cyril St. Clair was down there right now, scratching his head in response to whatever had happened.

Arthur turned to her, the amused expression still on his face. "You know, if you want to go see what's happening, you can. The car's not really going anywhere."

Clémence shook her head. "No. What good would it do? There's already a whole crowd over there. What's the point in joining that crazy mob?"

"Okay." Arthur arched an eyebrow. "You just look like you're dying to find out, that's all."

The corner of his mouth was twitching. Was he trying to suppress his laughter? Clémence scowled. Why did her boyfriend have to know her so well?

The taxi driver had the radio on. It had been playing frenetic jazz on low until a breaking-news segment came on. Clémence asked him to turn it up.

"We've just heard that a body has been found in the Seine River, near Pont Alexandre III. The body had been discovered by a local jogger around noon. The identity of the victim is still unknown, as is the cause of death."

Clémence couldn't stand it any longer–she got out of the car.

As she approached the crowd, she noticed some of the people were trying to film what was going on down at the Seine on their smartphones. Others were distraught, comforting each other. They were sectioned off by the police from the scene of the crime down by the riverbank.

Clémence stood on her tippy-toes to try to see, but she couldn't push through the crowd.

"What happened down there?" Clémence asked a bespectacled man in his forties who was tall enough to see over the few heads before them.

"A woman drowned in the Seine," he answered. "Apparently she's an actress."

A brunette teenage girl turned around. "Not just any actress. It's Nicole Blake."

"Nicole Blake?" Clémence exclaimed. "I didn't even know she was in Paris."

"Yeah, she was filming some sort of drama."

"Are you sure it's her?"

The girl shrugged. "Dunno. But that's what some people are saying. They have her in a body bag now."

Clémence clasped a hand over her mouth. She loved Nicole Blake's films. The twenty-four-year-old had been acting since she was fifteen, and her star had been on the rise in the last few years, when she developed killer curves. Not only was she beautiful, but she was talented enough to be nominated for an Oscar for best supporting actress last year for her role as a president's daughter in a political thriller.

"It's a shame," the teenaged boy beside the brunette girl commented. "She was hot."

The girl rolled her eyes at him.

"What happened?" Clémence asked.

The girl shrugged. "Nobody knows. Maybe she fell in, maybe she was pushed."

"So it might be murder," Clémence muttered.

She quickly shook her head to clear away her thoughts. She wasn't going back into investigative mode again, not when she'd barely returned home.

A few people in front of her left, and she was able to look down at the riverbank.

The ambulance workers were pushing a gurney into the back of the ambulance. The body bag on top of the gurney was closed.

Then she saw the slim figure of Inspector Cyril St. Clair. As she had imagined, he was stroking his chin, looking puzzled by the situation.

Chapter 2

The next day, Clémence tried to block out any thoughts of the recent death in Paris. In the afternoon, she decided to set up her easel on her balcony again. While a few gray clouds were hanging over her head, the sky was lit up enough that she could paint with natural light and enjoy what was left of the summer weather.

Her artistic ambition had been reignited after visiting the wonderful museums in Amsterdam. She and Arthur had passed a full afternoon at the Van Gogh museum, where they were mesmerized by the vibrant brushstrokes of his masterpieces. Her favorite had been his self-portraits, where he always looked slightly lost, his dark eyes haunted.

They'd gone to the Rijksmuseum the next day to look at paintings of the old Dutch masters, then Stedelijk Museum for modern art. Clémence had neglected her desire to paint for too long. She'd even signed up for experimental art classes so she could discover her own painting style, but classes were on hiatus for the month of August. Even when classes were in session, she'd had to miss most of the classes she'd paid for due to the murder cases that had taken up most of her time.

As she began painting again, she realized that her style had emerged after all. She was beginning to feel satisfied with the whimsical style she'd adopted in the past few months. She used pastel hues, which gave the work a happy aura. With Miffy sniffing at her heels, she painted three Damour chocolate éclairs with a blue sky as a backdrop, giving the éclairs the impression that they were light enough to float.

So her subjects weren't exactly deep enough to warrant a thought-provoking description. But she had decided that if she painted what she liked, the passion would come across in her work. For too long, she'd painted things she wasn't passionate about in order to be taken seriously and along the way, she'd lost her creative passion. Now, at the age of twenty-nine, she was reclaiming the original magic that had made her want to be a painter as a child.

Wearing paint-splattered overalls and a straw fedora to protect her porcelain skin from the sun, she continued chipping away at the éclairs, and hours passed like minutes. During that time, Arthur came home from work early. Since many of his coworkers were still on vacation, the office wasn't as busy as it usually was. When he poked his head out on the balcony, Clémence stopped what she was doing. She couldn't paint with people looking over her shoulder–she supposed she was still shy about her creative process.

She looked at her watch. It was almost time for Ben and Berenice to come over anyway. She didn't want everyone commenting on her work just yet, so she moved the painting to one end of the balcony, away from view, for it to dry.

It was almost five thirty when the couple came. Ben lived upstairs in a *chambre de bonne*, an old servant's room, which was on the top floor of the Haussmanian building. Berenice must've been hanging out with him in his tiny apartment because they both came down through the kitchen door, which opened to the old servants' staircase leading up to the top floor. Clémence led them straight out to the balcony. It usually rained all year round in Paris, and they had to grab any sunshine they could. Even in August, the city rarely got humid, but that afternoon was hotter than usual. Since the building didn't have air conditioning, Clémence opened many of her windows to let the air flow in.

Berenice brought two strawberry white-wine coolers, which were good for the late summer afternoon. Arthur helped her put the bottles in an ice bucket, and they brought out wine glasses to the balcony.

Berenice also brought some macarons, rejects from her shift as a baker at Damour. She smelled like the kitchen, full of sweets and cinnamon. It was how Clémence smelled whenever she got off a shift at Damour. She'd been immune to the smell herself until she started dating Arthur, who always made comments about it. He would bite her neck and tell her that she was sweet enough to eat.

"Oh Berenice," Clémence sighed in jest when Berenice opened the Tupperware of pastel treats. "You just have to tempt me with macarons when I haven't even gone back to work yet."

"You don't *have* to eat them." Berenice grinned. "They're for everybody."

The box contained Damour's pistachio, raspberry, and chocolate macarons. While they tasted the same as regular Damour macarons, they were deformed in some way, whether cracked at the shell or shaped funny. Damour didn't sell any macarons that looked or tasted less than perfect. Still, the macarons looked delicious, however misshapen. Clémence couldn't resist for long.

"Oh, give me one." She reached for a chocolate one and quickly bit into it.

The boys chuckled.

"You're an addict," Arthur said. "I bet you can't last a week without eating a macaron or a *pain au chocolat*."

"Well, we don't have to worry about that," Clémence replied, licking her fingers. "I have no choice but to eat plenty of sweets because I'm in the kitchen five or six days a week."

"You didn't have that excuse when we were on vacation." He turned to the couple. "Clémence was still going into different patisseries and buying all kinds of desserts."

"Yeah, but you're supposed to try new things when you're on vacation. Plus, it's research."

"Clémence ate a lot of Dutch waffles," Arthur said.

"They have pretty good ice cream and pies too," Clémence said brightly. "But we also did plenty of biking, so I think I actually lost weight."

"What else did you guys do?" Ben asked.

"My sister Marianne joined us when we were in Normandy for a few days," Clémence said. "She was pretty happy to get a few days away from her kids. We spent some time at the beach. My brother Henri and his family didn't live far, so we all went to visit him for the day too."

"So I finally met her siblings," Arthur said.

"I wish they'd spend more time in Paris," Clémence added, "but they're so busy."

"Well, I don't think Henri likes Paris very much."

"Right, he always goes on these rants about how Paris is crowded, dirty, and full of tourists. He's just not a city guy."

"Did you guys end up going on vacation?" Arthur asked Ben and Berenice.

"I wouldn't call going back to London a vacation," Ben, who was English, said. "But yeah, Berenice spent a few days there. My mom gave her an astrology reading."

Ben's mother was a well-known astrologer who often did readings for celebrities.

"No way!" Clémence exclaimed. "Was it accurate?"

"Startlingly so," Berenice said. "She also made some predictions. I'll tell you about it later."

"She won't tell me anything," Ben said. "My mom won't either, staying loyal to client confidentiality."

"I can't wait." Clémence grinned at Berenice mischievously. She wondered if Ben's mom had said anything about their relationship and whether she and Ben would get married or not.

"Hey, did you guys hear about the actress who drowned in the Seine?" Ben asked. "I read about it on my Twitter feed today."

"We did," Clémence said. "They just confirmed it was Nicole Blake this morning. How sad."

"We were actually driving past the scene when they found her body in the Seine," Arthur said.

"It's unfortunate," Clémence added. "I loved her in *Peach State*."

Peach State was one of Clémence's favorite movies. It was about a small-town restaurant owner and baker played by Nicole Blake. It was a sweet romantic comedy where Nicole's character played matchmaker to many of her regular customers before finding love with the local veterinarian.

"That was a cute movie," Berenice said. "Did they say why she drowned?"

"I don't know," Clémence said. "The papers didn't say. Was she on a boat? I have no idea."

"There's some speculation that Nicole Blake had some sort of drinking problem," Ben said.

"She *is* rumored to be somewhat of a diva," Berenice said. "Especially since she got her Oscar nod. I've been reading stories in the papers about her not getting along with her co-stars on the movie she's filming here."

"Did the film wrap already?" Arthur asked.

"No," Berenice said. "They were halfway done. There were all these filming delays. I heard that they have to give more scenes to Sarah Briar now that Nicole's not able to shoot the rest."

"Who's Sarah Briar playing?" Clémence asked. She hadn't been keeping up with the news in Paris since she'd been away.

"Nicole Blake's older sister. The film's about two American sisters who come to Paris after they've inherited an apartment in Montmartre and a valuable painting. Nicole had a bigger role and a meatier storyline, but now I heard they're forced to do without some of Nicole's scenes, and they're writing in more scenes for Sarah's character."

"That sounds pretty suspect, doesn't it?" Clémence said.

"What? You think Sarah Briar killed Nicole Blake?" Ben asked.

"I don't know," Clémence said. "But I'd consider that angle."

"That is, if Nicole was even killed," Berenice said.

"True," Clémence agreed.

"Why don't you snoop around on set and find out," Arthur suggested wryly.

Clémence shook her head. "No way. No more murder cases. If it's even a murder. It could be an accident, you know. This incident has nothing to do with me, or Damour, so I'm just going to let the police handle it this time."

"Really?" Berenice said. "You're not the least bit curious about what happened?"

"Curious, sure, but enough to spend time with that inspector?"

"I thought you loved getting on his nerves," Arthur said.

“That’s always fun, but if I had an option to not have to deal with him or any more dead bodies, I’d take it.”

“Oh, I don’t know,” Berenice said. “I think you like solving cases, and you’re good at it. And I think you have an in on the film set. Sophie Seydoux is making a small cameo as the girlfriend of one of the character’s love interests.”

“Really?” Clémence asked.

“Yup. I’m sure she could get you on set and introduce you to the cast and crew if you’d ask her.”

Once again, Clémence shook her head resolutely. She downed her glass of white wine cooler.

“Nope. I will not get involved this time. Definitely not.”

Chapter 3

After two weeks of being away from the Damour kitchen at 4 Place du Trocadéro, Clémence felt happy to be back. After greeting the staff, including the busy chefs and bakers in the kitchen, she settled in at the work table that she shared with Berenice and her brother Sebastien. Sebastien was Damour's head baker, whom she often worked with to invent new dessert flavors.

He was working on a new madeleine flavor, Raspberry and Rose, when Clémence came in. Together, they worked on three separate batches to improve on the recipe until they decided that the third one was perfect.

Celine, one of the hostesses in the *salon de thé*, came in to chat during her break as they were indulging themselves with the new madeleines.

"Don't mind if I do." Celine took a warm madeleine and bit into it. "*C'est très très bon.*"

"*Merci.*" Sebastien looked a little too proud. "We've outdone ourselves. It's not too fruity, with just a hint of the rose."

"Hey, I forgot to tell you," Celine said to Clémence. "When you were away, some of the stars from that Hollywood film, *The Art of Amour*, were here. Nicole Blake was here all the time, and so was Sarah Briar, although never together. They were shooting a lot in the neighborhood for about a week and a half. It was so exciting! I got to watch Zach film a kissing scene with Nicole outside La Coquette. Well, you know, it was before Nicole Blake died."

"Oh, that's right," Berenice said. "The patisserie cashiers told me that a couple of crew members would come in and buy massive amounts of desserts and pastries to go for the set."

"If I'd known," Clémence said, "I would've offered to give them a special discount on catering on the set."

"Well, they've already moved on to shooting scenes in other parts of the city," Celine said. "I think they're in Montmartre now. Too bad. Zach Brant is perfection."

"Is that guy ever fully clothed in a movie?" Sebastien quipped.

"*Pourquoi?*" Clémence asked. "Are you only interested when he's not?"

Sebastien snorted. "He played a gigolo in his last movie and walked around naked in ninety percent of the scenes. He's not big because he can act, that's for sure."

"Oh please," Berenice said. "As if women aren't objectified in movies all the time. It's refreshing for the girls to get some visual action for a change."

"Hey, Zach Brant just broke up with that mousy actress," Celine said. "He's single again."

"Are you going to stalk him until he notices you?" Clémence smiled.

"Oh, he already has. After one of his takes, we made eye contact. Like, full-on eye contact for at least three seconds. It was intense. But they kept asking him to redo the takes, and after he wrapped, the bodyguards ushered the crowd away, and the actors disappeared into a van. I saw him looking around before he ducked into the van, so he might've been looking for me."

Sebastien laughed. "Eye contact? How far away were you? He was probably just staring into space and trying to remember his lines."

"Whatever," Celine said. "I'm telling you, we had a moment. When I'm walking down the red carpet, arm linked with his, we'll see who has the last laugh."

She turned on her heels and walked out the door in a huff.

Sebastien shook his head. "Delusional as always."

"She's a dreamer," Clémence said. "I kind of admire that."

"Zach Brant *is* pretty hot," Berenice said. "You could wash laundry on those abs."

"Ugh." Sebastien put in his earbuds and turned on his iPod. "After you finish discussing the rest of his body parts, let me know."

Clémence and Berenice laughed. Sebastien could be so uptight sometimes.

The *salon de thé* was extra busy during lunch since the Parisians were starting to return from vacation. All the tables inside and on the terrace were full. Customers needed reservations to get a table. Clémence helped Celine and another hostess deal with the lineup. They had to turn away a lot of people, mainly tourists who didn't realize they needed to call ahead to get a table. They were encouraged to go to the patisserie, where they could at least take away some famous Damour treats to go so their trip wasn't a total loss.

They were still dealing with the lunch rush when a young woman wearing black-rimmed glasses cut the line to talk to one of the hostesses.

"Do you have a reservation?" Celine asked her.

"*Non, desolée*," the young woman said in an American accent. "I'm not here to eat. Is it possible to see Clémence? Clémence Damour?"

Clémence had been within earshot, chatting with a regular customer. She turned around to face the American.

"I'm Clémence. Can I help you?"

"Hi. I'm sorry to bother you at such a busy time, but I heard I could find you here, and I'd like to speak to you in private about an important matter."

Clémence sized up the young woman. She had a plain-Jane quality about her. Her brown hair in a ponytail, and her face completely devoid of makeup. She had a smattering of freckles on her face, and she couldn't have been over twenty-five. Her French was a bit awkward, high school level, but it was competent enough.

"Is it urgent?" Clémence asked.

The young woman nodded. She stepped to the side, away from the lineup and closer to Clémence so the others couldn't hear.

"It's regarding Nicole Blake's death. I was her assistant."

Clémence slowly nodded. "I see."

She looked around. Carolyn was coming out of her office and walking toward them. Clémence asked her to fill in for her.

"Why don't you come with me to the back?" Clémence told the American.

The young woman followed Clémence past the tables of the salon into the back section. They turned to the right and reached Carolyn's empty office. When they were both inside, Clémence closed the door behind them.

"Please sit." Clémence gestured to a chair as she sat behind Carolyn's desk.

"*Je m'appelle Rachel.*" Her voice sounded shakier now that they were alone in a quiet room.

"We can speak English if you prefer," Clémence offered.

"Oh, that would be great." Rachel sighed in relief. "My French is usually okay, but it would be easier to speak in English for this matter. I'm a bit nervous."

"You must be shaken after Nicole's death."

Rachel nodded solemnly. "It was definitely a shock."

"Were you her personal assistant?"

"No, not exactly. I was interning for Harper Studios, which is making *The Art of Amour*. Are you familiar with the film? They've been shooting here in Paris for the past few weeks. You know, the one Nicole Blake was starring in?"

"Yes, I'm aware."

"Well, the studio assigned me to be Nicole's assistant on this film because her own assistants kept quitting on her. Nicole didn't want another assistant at first, but the producers insisted. I guess they wanted me to keep an eye on her here. In a way, I was a glorified babysitter, but I'd come to like

Nicole. She was prickly at first, but through this experience on set in Paris, we'd become friends, almost. I feel guilty that she died on my watch."

"Why are you here to see me?" Clémence asked.

"Sophie Seydoux recommended that I speak to you. She says you're good at digging out the truth."

"Really?" Clémence raised an eyebrow. "What exactly is the problem?"

"I think Nicole Blake might've been murdered."

Chapter 4

Clémence caught her breath. "How do you know? *What* do you know?"

Rachel took out an agenda from her black purse. "This is Nicole's agenda. She's so secretive that she wrote a lot of it in a secret code."

Clémence took the red leather agenda from Rachel's frail fingers. She unhooked the metallic clasp. "I didn't know people still used these."

"Well, Nicole had been paranoid about technology ever since somebody hacked into her phone."

"Right," Clémence said. "I remember her topless photo scandal, but those kinds of things are not a huge deal in France."

"Nicole had a good PR company, and it did blow over, but she'd been paranoid ever since. She avoids texting anything personal, and the same goes for emails. In a way her extreme privacy backfired, because her death is a secret as well. The police are having a hard time figuring out what happened to her. They might rule it as an accident."

"Why are you coming to me with this agenda?" Clémence asked. "It could be a vital clue. Why don't you go to the police?"

"I thought about it." Rachel twisted the hem of her cotton button-down shirt. "I lived in Paris for a semester for exchange when I was in my third year of university. Once, my purse was stolen when I was in a bar, and the police basically laughed at me when I reported it and asked whether they'd be able to help me get my stuff back. I've heard other stories about the police from my French friends as well. And with the clumsy investigation I've witnessed so far, I just don't have any faith in them."

Clémence nodded. "I really don't blame you." She thought about the clueless Inspector Cyril St. Clair. He couldn't think his way out of a paper bag.

"Sophie told me about what you did when she was kidnapped," Rachel said. "She says you're clever, and you'd do a much better job than the professionals. What do you think? Can you help?"

"I want to." Clémence turned the pages, frowning at the indecipherable letters. "But this is in code, and I've never decoded anything before. What do you think is in here that would prove that Nicole was murdered?"

"Where she was and who she was with last Saturday, for example, the night before her body was found." Rachel helped her flip to the page. "Here. It says 'Meeting with OVUJOV.'"

"Ovujov? What could that be?" Clémence remarked. "Why does she only write certain things in code and not others?"

"She does it for important meetings that she doesn't want anyone to know about. See her appointments for hair salons and manicures?"

"It's in plain English." Clémence nodded. "It's impressive. She was that private, huh?"

"She hates computers and technology now. The phone-hacking incident had been really humiliating for her. Not so much that her nudes were leaked and tainted her image. She doesn't like things to be beyond her control. And for some anonymous hacker to gain access to all her information was a lot to bear. She often said she wanted to live in the sixties, when everybody used typewriters. She hates the internet, and would avoid it like the plague, although I've caught her Googling herself more than once."

"The internet is a vicious black hole." Clémence could sympathize. There were plenty of horrible articles and blog posts written about her online. "When was the last time you saw Nicole?"

"At the hotel. The cast and crew are all staying at the Athena Hotel."

"Oh, that's not far from here."

"Yes. The actors, the directors, and the producers are in suites, so they're on a different floor. The rest of us are in regular rooms. I'm lucky to get my own room, since others have to share. It was Nicole's doing. She insisted I get my own room and have it be close to hers, but they couldn't manage that, since they didn't want to spring for a luxury suite for an assistant." Rachel shrugged. "The night before she was found dead, she was in my room before she went out, and we had been going over her lines for the next day."

"Is that why you got your own room? So she could come over?"

"Yes. I was only allowed into her room to do specific things, like organize her closet. Otherwise, she came to my room. Nobody else could go into her room. She was that private."

"What time did she leave?"

"It was about ten thirty p.m., which was late. We were in my room for hours. She was snacking a lot. She kept eating madeleines—they were from Damour, by the way. The crew bought a lot of Damour items, and she became obsessed with the madeleines. It's funny, now that I'm here talking to you, the heiress of Damour."

"What kind of madeleines?" Clémence knew she was getting off topic, but she was curious.

"The almond praliné ones," Rachel replied. "I remembered because she brought them into my room and offered some to me. She said she always ate Damour madeleines when she was in Paris."

"The almond pralinés were a new flavor," Clémence muttered. She tried to imagine Nicole Blake stuffing her face with her madeleines and smiled.

"She did need to watch her figure, but she argued that the madeleines weren't as fattening as the other Damour desserts, so she felt as if she could indulge. But that night she was wolfing them back like there was no tomorrow. Maybe she was nervous, because I'd never seen her eat so much so fast."

"It's unfortunate that my madeleines were the last thing she probably ate before she died." Clémence sighed. Were her products really cursed?

"Considering that Nicole's call time the following morning was at six a.m., wherever she was going must've been pretty important," Rachel said.

Clémence looked at Nicole's agenda again. The coded appointment was written beside the 10:30 p.m. slot.

"She gets into this zone when she rehearses with me sometimes," Rachel said. "After half an hour, she stopped snacking and really got into her scenes. I don't care what anyone says about her. She was the most talented actress of our generation. We both lost track of time as she worked, and when she glanced at her watch at around ten thirty, she practically jumped out of her chair. She grabbed her clutch and said she had to go run an errand."

"That was all she said?"

"Yes. She just ran out. She was in a huge rush, and I didn't have time to ask her anything else. But she left her script behind, and her agenda, which she'd carried in a separate Gucci tote bag. She had her clutch that contained her phone and keys with her, which still hasn't been found. The police are saying that it was a mugging. Or the clutch is at the bottom of the Seine."

Clémence sighed. "I suppose you're right about the agenda. It's our best bet to find out where she'd gone. But tell me, is it true that she had a drinking problem?"

"I think she used to, when she was a teenager. Whenever the crew went out to dinner, she never drank alcohol, which gave me the impression that she was trying hard not to fall off the bandwagon. She never told me she was in AA, but it was clear she had issues with alcohol in the past. I assumed she was trying to keep on a straight path."

"So you don't think she could've been drinking that night?" Clémence asked.

"No. I'm sure she wasn't. Unless she drank with someone else that night."

"What if it was an accident?" Clémence said. "What if she only went out with a friend, went crazy on the drinks, and maybe fell in the Seine on her way home. It is a possibility."

"Nicole's a great swimmer. When we were shooting in L.A., we were shooting at a beach house, and she'd swim in the ocean on her off days, no problem. She even knew how to surf. There's no way that she wouldn't have been able to handle the Seine, even if she had been drunk, which I doubt. I don't believe the rumors that blame alcohol or drugs for landing her in the river."

"You said Nicole was nervous that evening. Why do you think she was nervous?"

"I don't know. It wasn't unusual to see her that way. I rarely saw her relaxed, in fact. But actually, when she was jumping to leave, I thought she seemed happy to go. Excited even."

"Was she dating anyone?"

"That's the thing. I don't know much about her private life. She wouldn't tell me. I did get the impression that she was, because sometimes she'd get a text and she'd have a dreamy smile on her face, or she'd laugh. Since her phone was lost, we don't have a way of knowing who she'd been in contact with."

"Do you think anyone would have enough motive to kill her?"

"Well, Nicole didn't exactly get along with her co-stars. It wasn't a secret. It's true that Nicole could be a diva sometimes. That was Nicole's fault. She'd either decide she liked you and would charm your pants off, or she'd treat you as if you weren't fit to be the gum on the bottom of her shoe."

Clémence nodded. "I heard that Sarah Briar didn't get along with her."

"They didn't at all. Sarah turned thirty-four recently, and Nicole was starting to get the kinds of roles she used to get. Nicole was the director's favorite too, and she had first pick of wardrobe. Sarah just never spoke to her unless they had to do a scene together. It could get pretty awkward on set."

"Did anyone else hate her?"

"Zach Brant. He was playing Nicole's love interest in the movie, but they just couldn't stand each other. The funny thing is, once the cameras were rolling, you could've sworn they were in love. But otherwise, they often made jabs at each other. Zach thought Nicole was a complete monster, and Nicole taunted him for his bad acting, among other things. The truth is, Zach isn't the best actor. He's okay playing the handsome male lead where he has to look pretty, but in the emotional scenes, Zach could barely keep up with Nicole, who could cry on demand. At first I thought their feud was because of some sort of romantic tension, given the amount of time Nicole would rant about him to me. I don't know. What girl could resist Zach Brant? But after talking to Zach, I realized he genuinely didn't like her either. Besides, he had a long-term girlfriend."

"I'd like to talk to Zach and Sarah individually," Clémence said.

"I'll get you an introduction," Rachel said. "Now that Nicole's, you know, off the project, I'm working for Sarah Briar as her assistant. She didn't have one before."

"Cool."

Rachel rolled her eyes. "I don't know about that. Nicole never liked her, and she does seem quite—oh, what am I saying? Honestly, I don't know Sarah Briar that well. Maybe I have Stockholm syndrome after working for Nicole."

"Well, let's exchange numbers," Clémence said. "Keep me informed, and let me know when's a good time to visit the set. In the meantime, I'll try to decode this thing."

"Sure." Rachel took out her phone, and she keyed in Clémence's number. "And if you have any questions, you can always call or text me."

"Where are you shooting now?"

"In a house in Montmartre, where the characters are supposed to be living. They also rented out a house across the street for the cast and crew to rest in between takes. We just started."

"What's going to happen to Nicole's hotel room? Have police gone through it?"

"Yes," Rachel said. "They went through her belongings. They found nothing, so all her designer clothes, bags, and shoes are still there. Her family's supposed to get back to me as to whether they want her things back. Otherwise, we're going to donate her things to charity."

"Wait, do you have access to her room?"

"Yes. I do have her key. She left it behind in her Gucci tote."

"Get me in there," Clémence said with excitement.

Chapter 5

Clémence made plans to meet with Rachel at the Athena Hotel the next morning. Most of the cast and crew would be on location shooting the film, so Rachel would be able to sneak her into Nicole's room. Whenever she was investigating a case, she found it difficult to bake at Damour, to paint—or to do anything, really. The only thing she could do was relax a bit before her 10:00 a.m. appointment by taking Miffy for a walk at Champ de Mars.

She'd stayed up for a couple of hours, trying to decode Nicole's agenda. She thought the words might've been anagrams, so she tried rearranging the letters of a few coded words. That didn't work. It couldn't have been Pig Latin because the words didn't end with -ay. Had it been Nicole's own brand of gibberish that she made up so no one else could understand it?

It wasn't an advantage that only a small portion of the content was written in code. If the entire agenda had been in code, she could've figured out where Nicole had been in the appointed times.

Even figuring out one event could've helped her decode everything else.

In August, there were two different codes: "OVUJOV" and "ILILIL".

"OVUJOV" had appeared twelve times in her book that month. Four of them were in the mornings, at sporadic times, but never after nine a.m. It was probably because Nicole had to shoot her film. The other four took place in the evenings, anywhere from nine thirty to eleven. "ILILIL" had only appeared once, in an afternoon slot. Was it a person? A place? The entry had simply said, "Visit ILILIL."

When she saw Rachel, she had to ask for Nicole's filming schedule.

Once Clémence and Miffy reached Champ de Mars, Miffy began running. She pulled at her leash, and Clémence decided to run with her. She felt the cool air against her skin; autumn was definitely on its way. The leaves of the neatly trimmed trees that lined either side of the park were already changing colors. There were still a lot of tourists, but the park felt more peaceful since it was an early weekday morning. There were some people who were picnicking on the grass already, as well as locals reading newspapers and books on the benches.

She kept up with Miffy at a jogging pace, glad that she'd worn comfortable quilted black Chanel flats that morning. She laughed as Miffy dragged her from bush to flower to tree. Sometimes Miffy was too curious of a dog; she'd put anything in her mouth. Clémence had to drag her away from a bag of pretzels that had been spilled on the ground. One of the reasons why she hardly ever took Miffy into Damour was that sometimes the customers wanted to feed her. Once, a sweet old lady almost managed to give Miffy a piece of a chocolate éclair. Chocolate was lethal for dogs, and Miffy could've been a goner if Clémence hadn't come to the rescue.

As she looked around the peaceful park, she felt a tinge of sadness that summer was ending. While the murders around Paris had caused a lot of stress and chaos, she'd had the best summer of her life with Arthur and all of her friends. She took a deep breath, taking in the fresh air that was already tinged with autumn's crispness, and then began walking back to her home.

After she dropped Miffy off in the living room to play with her toys in a corner, Clémence left for the Athena Hotel. The luxury hotel was only a ten-minute walk from her place, so she walked some more. Clémence didn't mind the exercise. Her thighs had gotten stronger after all the biking in the Netherlands, plus now that she was back working at Damour, she was surely going to be eating more sweets, so any exercise was good in her book.

The Athena Hotel had beautiful red flowers on every balcony, and as Clémence approached, she couldn't help but look up to admire the vivid color against the beige facade. Some of her friends and distant relatives stayed at the four-star hotel whenever they visited her in Paris. Clémence had drunk in the hotel's famous Blue Bar, its high class but cozy bar with plush, blue velvet seats and mahogany walls adorned with black and white headshots of movie stars from the golden age.

As Clémence walked, she texted Rachel to confirm that she was coming, but Rachel didn't text back. They had made the rendezvous only yesterday, so Clémence assumed Rachel would keep her word. Rachel had already given her the room number she was staying in, so Clémence could go there directly.

Passing porters in elegant red uniforms trimmed with gold, and smartly dressed hotel staff, Clémence took the elevator to the third floor.

She knocked on the door of room 305 and waited. After a few seconds passed, Rachel didn't come to the door, so Clémence called her on the phone.

She heard the phone ring on the other side of the door. It kept ringing and ringing. Clémence wondered if Rachel had been called onto the set at the last minute and had forgotten her phone at home.

If Clémence had known where exactly they were filming, going there might've been an option. Since she didn't, she decided to go back downstairs and wait in case Rachel were to come back. Since Clémence was already at the Athena, she could have a drink at the Blue Bar and try to search the gossip blogs on her phone to see where the crew was shooting.

When the elevator door opened on the ground floor, Clémence came out and ran into a young woman with a short pixie haircut. The woman had a precious face with large doe eyes and dimples.

"Clémence!" Sophie Seydoux exclaimed.

"*Salut*, Sophie." Clémence greeted her with a *bisou* on each cheek.

Sophie was heiress to the famous gourmet chocolate stores, *Chateau du Chocolat*, along with her sister Madeleine. They were both It girls and socialites who were often stalked by the paparazzi and appeared in fashion and tabloid magazines. After Sophie's infamous kidnapping incident, their fame rubbed off on Clémence for a while before the paparazzi got tired of her boring life and got distracted by the real celebrities who'd shown up in Paris for the summer to shoot Hollywood films.

Clémence was now good friends with both Seydoux sisters. She was starting to lunch with them quite frequently before she went on summer vacation.

After they exchanged pleasantries about their summer escapades, Clémence congratulated Sophie on her role in the film.

"It's not a major part," Sophie said modestly.

"I heard you're playing Zach Brant's girlfriend, right?" Clémence said with a sly smile.

"Yes, and we don't even have a kissing scene." Sophie laughed. "I shot two scenes with him and that was it."

"So what are you doing here? You're not dating him now, are you?"

"Oh, no. Don't believe those rumors," Sophie said. "Actually, I'm here to meet with the director. Since Nicole Blake, well, passed away, he and the writers had to change the script. He wanted to talk to me about expanding my role."

"Congrats," Clémence said. "You're going to be a movie star in no time."

"I always wanted to act, but it's a bit funny getting a bigger role as a result of someone else's tragedy, you know? Poor Nicole."

"Did you know her well?"

"Not really. She was in one of the two scenes that I shot. She was pleasant enough but didn't take an active interest in me or anything. Then again, Nicole had a full shooting schedule, and she seemed to be very busy and distracted."

"Her assistant came to visit me yesterday," Clémence said. "She said you recommended that she speak to me?"

"Oh yes, Rachel. She's sweet, isn't she? She told me that she thought Nicole was murdered. I didn't know what to think about that, but I figured she'd benefit from talking to you. I figured if anything, you would be able to help more than the police would. What do you think so far?"

"Not too much," Clémence said. "But I'm supposed to be meeting Rachel now. Any idea where she is? She's not in her hotel room."

"And you tried calling her?"

"Yes. She left her phone in the hotel room. Do you think she's on set?"

"Well, I don't know. I'm meeting with Chris now, so they must not be shooting, unless the second unit director is shooting some B-roll of the streets. Maybe Rachel's doing some errands for Sarah Briar now that she's working for her. I know that Chris is supposed to be on set in another hour or so, after our meeting."

"Okay," Clémence said. "That makes sense if Rachel left to help Sarah. But maybe you can help.

I want to talk to some of the cast to learn more about Nicole."

"Why don't you come meet Chris? I'm going to have a chat, but if you wait outside, I can make an introduction after I'm done."

"That would be great."

"Let's get in the elevator," Sophie said when one became available. "I don't want to be late. Chris hates tardiness."

"I've seen his work," Clémence said. "At least a couple of his films. He's very versatile, isn't he?"

"Yeah, I enjoyed working with him. He was so on top of everything. Then again, I haven't worked on many films to compare."

On the sixth floor, Clémence waited in the hall when Sophie went in. She tried calling Rachel again, only to get the voicemail. Clémence texted her to let her know she was still in the hotel, in case she did happen to go home for her phone.

As Clémence waited, she read the newspaper articles about Nicole Blake's death on her smart-phone. A recent article said that her pink Chloe purse had been found by a local. It had been floating near the edge of the Seine near Notre Dame. The purse had been empty, the contents probably scattered around the bottom of the Seine. They were still awaiting autopsy results; the cause of death was still unknown.

"Clémence?" Sophie poked her heart-shaped face out the door and smiled. "Come on in."

Chapter 6

Chris Collins's suite was practically the size of Clémence's own apartment. It must've been a family suite. The director was sitting on one of the black leather couches in the living room. He faced the windows, which had a view of the rooftops of Paris. When Clémence approached, he stood up to greet her. At six foot two, he was quite a bit taller than Clémence's five-foot-four frame, and as he shook her hand, she felt as if she was a kid being looked down on by a grownup. He had dirty blond hair and green eyes framed by thick lashes, and while not movie-star handsome, he was someone Celine would definitely find chase-worthy. But then again, Celine wasn't the pickiest girl in the world when it came to men.

Clémence knew that Chris had started directing movies only four years ago. Now at thirty-seven, he was finally making a name for himself in the industry.

"Hi, I'm Clémence," she said in English.

He smiled broadly, in his American way. "Chris Collins." He shook her hand. "*Enchanté*. My French is still bad even after all these weeks here. Where's my translator when I need her?" He let out an easygoing laugh.

"Nice to meet you too, Monsieur Collins," Clémence said.

"Call me Chris. *S'il vous plait–*" He gestured the seats in the spacious living room. "Please sit." Clémence took the single sofa next to his couch. Sophie sat in another single sofa beside her. "Sophie tells me you're the Clémence Damour of the Damour patisseries? Your family's famous among my crew. We're all obsessed with your macarons and pastries."

"So I've heard." Clémence smiled back. She felt a surge of pride every time she received a compliment about the Damour desserts.

"Personally, I'm addicted to your *millefeuilles.* I can't believe I haven't had one before coming to Paris."

"If it's one thing Parisians are good for, it's the desserts."

"I'll say. Sophie tells me you wanted to meet me." He tilted his head, examining her. "Are you an actress?"

"*Moi? Mais, non,*" Clémence protested.

"You're not? I thought you wanted to talk because you were looking for a part in the movie. We're looking for someone to play Sophie's French friend in the film, now that her role has been expanded."

"I'm really not an actress."

"Neither was Sophie here, but now she's about to sign a contract for a supporting role."

"Sophie has talent, but I'm not cut out for the spotlight, trust me."

Chris was still examining her, as if she were a rare jewel he had to authenticate. Being examined made her squirm, which was precisely why she didn't want to be back in the limelight.

"That's too bad," he said. "You have the bone structure for the big screen, and your features are certainly striking."

"Thanks," Clémence replied modestly.

Clémence had blue eyes that others, like Arthur, called electric since they were such a vivid blue. She had a dark, almost black bob and porcelain skin. She was no better looking than most women walking down the streets of Paris, but she was flattered nonetheless. A world-class director was telling her that she had potential to be a movie star. Who wouldn't get a big head from that?

"If you don't want to act, what did you want to talk to me about?" Chris asked.

"It's a sensitive issue, but, well, as you know, the circumstances surrounding Nicole Blake's death are a bit mysterious. I was wondering what you know about Ms. Blake."

Chris gave her an amused, mildly flirtatious smile. "I didn't know you also work for the French police, Mademoiselle Damour."

Clémence shifted uncomfortably. "Someone working on your set has reason to believe that Nicole Blake had been murdered. I thought you'd want to know so you can, well, keep an eye on things."

Chris raised an eyebrow. He was still amused and looking at her as if she was the most adorable thing in the world. "I don't think you have anything to worry about. I've worked with many of my crew members for years, and these movie stars aren't killers. We're like a big family. Sometimes we get mad at each other, and tensions can rise when we're in each other's company for too long, but that's normal for a film set."

"So you don't think that anybody had the motive to harm Nicole?" Clémence asked.

Chris sighed and shook his head. "Nicole...it's such a shame. She was wonderful to work with."

"Rumor has it that she could be difficult on set. Did you find that to be the case?"

"No. Nicole was always extremely professional. She knew all her lines and never wasted any film. She knew her angles; she was well trained. I mean, yes, sometimes she butted heads with the other actors, but it didn't necessarily affect the work. In fact, it might've made things better, since there was plenty of heat and chemistry in this drama."

"Have you ever seen her argue with her co-workers?"

"Well..." His eyes rolled to the ceiling as he contemplated the question. "She wasn't exactly warm and fuzzy with them offscreen. That's okay, as long as we get our work done. Ideally, I'd like everyone on set to get along and have a good time, like a family, but this industry is full of people with egos, and some actors don't come on set to make friends, which is fine. But to answer your question, no, I hadn't seen her argue with her coworkers myself. She'd always been professional on set."

"Could you tell that she didn't get along with certain cast or crew members?" Clémence asked.

"I don't know if she didn't get along with them, or just didn't have much of an interest in their lives, but Nicole didn't seem too...favorable towards Sarah Briar. They often went after the same roles. And Zach Brant. The ladies may love him, but Nicole wouldn't give him the time of day. He prides himself in charming every woman on set, but Nicole wouldn't have anything to do with him offscreen. But like I said, I don't care about personal matters as long as they have chemistry on screen. When the camera was on, Nicole really made you believe that she was deeply in love with Zach's character. She was a real actress." Chris grimaced and shook his head. "I'm sorry to lose her. Not only because the whole production is now upside down and needs to be rewritten, but we've lost a true artist."

Clémence nodded in sympathy "Was this your first time working with her?"

"Yes," said Chris.

He was about to continue when the front doors opened and a woman entered. Dressed in a pink Chanel skirt suit, she was a brunette in her early forties who resembled Jackie O. She was holding the hand of a little blond girl who looked to be about four while a boy around seven ran into the living room.

"Daddyyy!" he cried and jumped up into Chris's arms.

"Danny boy," Chris said, lifting him up into the air. Danny giggled.

The woman sashayed into the living room. The little girl looked shy, sucking on a thumb and peeking out at Clémence and Sophie from behind her mom.

"This is my wife Cynthia." Chris looked a bit uneasy. "Cynthia? You've met Sophie Seydoux before, right? And this is Clémence Damour. Her family owns the Damour patisserie."

Cynthia's dark eyes burned with annoyance at each girl as she sneered at them before turning her head back to her children. Clémence wanted to shiver as a result of her icy gaze.

"Oh, Damour," Cynthia said in a bored tone. "I tried to eat macarons with my tea there once, but honestly, darling, I prefer Pierre Hermé."

"Pierre Hermé is a friend of the family," Clémence said modestly. "I don't hold it against you for preferring his macarons. He's a genius, really."

Cynthia didn't seem interested in what she was saying.

"It looks like you're busy," Cynthia said coldly to her husband.

Chris stood up to kiss his wife. Even he seemed to be intimidated by her. "I'm just in the middle of a meeting, but it won't be long. How was the park?"

"Crowded. Cold. I don't know who's more dreadful, the Parisians or the tourists."

After giving Clémence and Sophie one last dirty look, Cynthia headed towards the double doors that presumably led into their bedrooms. "Come on, Danny."

The enthusiastic little boy followed after Cynthia and the little girl. The doors shut with a bang.

Chris gave them an awkward smile. "Sorry about the interruption."

"Your wife is—charming," Clémence said.

"Cynthia? Oh, yes. Sometimes she's a little intense, but she's still adjusting to Paris."

"Has she not been here for long?"

"She's been here with me throughout the shoot. Since school's out for Danny, my family's been able to stay here with me. I'm glad to have them here. They keep me grounded in this crazy showbiz."

"That's good to hear," Clémence said. "So back to Nicole Blake. Do you have any idea what could've happened to her?"

"Well I certainly don't think anybody on my production could've killed her. I work with them every day. I can't imagine someone I work with being a murderer."

"You'd be surprised how many seemingly innocent people turn out to be the perps of heinous crimes," Clémence said.

"You sound like someone who's seen a lot," Chris said, examining her again. "You're certainly a very interesting young woman. Are you sure there's no chance of you doing a cameo in my movie?"

"I'm afraid not." Clémence cracked a smile. "I'm just better behind the scenes."

"You know, I did talk to Nicole a lot about her character before we started shooting. We discussed the background of her character and how she was going to approach playing her. Her character is a recovering drug addict, and Nicole revealed to me that she was an alcoholic. What if she started drinking again?"

"Have you seen her drunk before?" Clémence asked.

"No. Never around me. But it's not as if we would go drinking together. I'm working around the clock, and I don't know what my cast and crew gets up to when they're not working."

"So that's what you think happened? She got drunk and had some sort of accident?"

"I hate to say it, but it's likely she fell off the wagon and went a bit overboard with alcohol. My uncle was an alcoholic. I've seen firsthand how difficult it is to quit drinking."

"I heard she'd been sober for years."

Chris sighed. He lowered his head, and the girls automatically leaned in. "This is not public knowledge, but Nicole was rejected last week for a role she really wanted. It was an Amelia Earhart biopic, and Nicole had been campaigning the director, who's a friend of mine, for months to get it. I put in a good word for her, but he took a pass. I'm afraid it was a blow to her ego I know that Nicole was set on winning an Oscar before she was thirty. The script would've given her a really good chance."

“So you think she took to drinking to take the edge off the rejection?” Clémence asked.

“It’s never easy. In my career, I have seen quite a number of actors taken by addiction. It’s a competitive industry, and actors are sensitive people to begin with. They need to be vulnerable to open themselves to the public like that. They have to, to make a living.”

Chapter 7

"So what do you think?" Sophie asked when they sat down in the Blue Bar of the Athena Hotel.

Clémence asked Caroline and Marie to help her dig up all the purchases and transaction information on their cash register before the store opened.

Clémence was craving a cocktail for some reason. Maybe it was all the talk about Nicole Blake's drinking problem. She and Sophie both ordered a Blue Haze, the Blue Bar's signature drink.

"I don't know," Clémence said. "Rachel thinks Nicole hadn't been drinking, but it would be plausible that Nicole would turn to the bottle if she was that upset about losing a plum role. But we still don't know who she had been meeting. And did this person kill her?"

"Contrary to what Chris said, I agree with you that there is potential that someone on our set would kill Nicole," Sophie said. "It's a competitive industry. Do you know how many other French actresses and models wanted my little cameo in this film? When I got it, some of these girls wouldn't talk to me at parties. Imagine that on a bigger scale, when you're one of the biggest stars in the world."

"That's true," Clémence agreed. "What's going on with Chris's wife? Is she always that rude?"

"I don't know what her problem is. I met her on set once when I was shooting a scene with Sarah Briar. Between takes, she came on set, and Chris introduced her to everyone. She seemed pleasant enough with most people, but when Chris introduced her to Sarah, Cynthia looked like she wanted to kill her. Same with me."

"So, what, she hates actresses?"

"I suppose she's not too happy about her husband working with attractive women all day long. She used to be a beauty back in the day, and she did some modeling, although she was never tall enough to gain supermodel status."

The bartender gave them their cocktails, and they both took a sip.

"I'll add Cynthia to the suspect list," Clémence said. "What does she do for a living now?"

"Not much," Sophie said. "She's a housewife, but she came from money. Her family owns Harper Studios. She met Chris because he was working for the studio."

"Wow, her family owns Harper Studios? Rich would be an understatement then."

"She was given a few opportunities to act when she was younger," Sophie said, "but she was a horrible actress. Had no charisma on screen. I've seen clips of one of the films on YouTube, and she was a laughingstock for a while. She even quit modeling because she was an embarrassment to the Harper name."

"Hmm. So she failed as a movie star, and now she's resentful of other young starlets. There's definitely some motive here. But it does sound like quite a few people had hated Nicole."

"Did Rachel ever respond to you?"

"I've been so distracted that I forgot I was supposed to meet her." Clémence took out her phone from her purse and turned on the screen. "No. She didn't reply at all."

She tried calling her again, but it only went to voicemail.

"You know what?" Sophie said. "I can call Sarah. I'm friends with her. They're not shooting scenes with the actors right now anyway."

She took out her phone and made the call. "Hey, Sarah?" After some small talk, she asked where Rachel was. "Really?...I'm sure that's not it, Sarah... well let me know if you see her."

When Sophie hung up, she had a strange look on her face.

"So where is Rachel?" Clémence asked.

"It's really odd. Rachel was supposed to meet Sarah this morning to go over some lines then help Sarah run some errands, but she never showed up. Sarah checked with the crew, and nobody knows where she is. Now Sarah thinks that Rachel's unhappy about being her assistant because she was so loyal to Nicole. She's pretty hurt because she thinks this is Rachel's way of saying she didn't want to work for her."

"I don't think that's the case," Clémence said, "considering that Rachel stood me up."

"I've met Rachel a few times, but she doesn't seem like the type to stand people up. She's very organized and diligent, definitely not the type to rebel, even if she was secretly unhappy about the Sarah situation."

"What if she's still in her hotel room?" Clémence said slowly. "Where else could she possibly be?"

"Why would she be there?" Sophie asked.

"I don't know, but I just think we should check just in case."

"Maybe she's still asleep. Or do you think she had an accident?"

"Come on, let's go talk to the concierge." Clémence got up from her stool.

They explained the situation to a young man behind the front desk with a name tag that said "Julien." At the sight of Sophie, his eyes widened. Since Sophie was more or less famous, he must've recognized her or found her to be beautiful, which she was.

"Sorry," Julien said bashfully. "I'm not allowed to let anyone in anyone else's suite."

"Please," Sophie pleaded. Her sweet face made Julien go soft. "It's a matter of life and death. My friend is missing, and she could be in trouble. Surely you'd want to help if she's in danger, wouldn't you? We just want to check her room to see if she's in there. We don't even have to go in. You can check for us."

"Well..." Julien looked between Sophie and Clémence's hopeful faces. He loosened up, seeming to make up his mind. "I do have access to the room. I guess it wouldn't hurt to quickly check."

"Thank you," Sophie breathed. "You're doing the right thing."

With the lovely lady's encouragement, Julien's chest puffed out like a cock's. He went into the back room and then emerged with a swipe card.

The three of them took the elevator up to the third floor. Before door 305, Julien knocked.

"*Madame?*" he called. "Anybody there?"

As expected, there was no answer. After knocking some more and receiving silence as a response, Julien swiped the card and pushed the door open.

He took a few steps inside. Then he let out a huge gasp, staggering back out into the hall.

“What is it?” Clémence asked.

Julien pointed. His lips shook, and he was unable to speak.

Clémence braced herself and walked in. She saw the source of his distress: Rachel’s body was swinging from a chandelier. A brown leather belt was looped around her neck, and the skin of her face and body had turned gray-blue.

“*Mon dieu!*” Sophie said behind Clémence. “Call the police!”

Chapter 8

"Are you okay, *chérie*?" Arthur asked when he returned home late from work.

He put his laptop bag on a side table in the living room and entered the salon, where Clémence was sitting on the couch, clutching a glass of red wine and staring into space. In front of her on the glass coffee table was her notebook full of her scribbled writing. She was so deep in her thoughts that it took a while for her to register Arthur's presence.

"What?" she asked after a long delay.

He glanced at the half-empty bottle of wine next to the notebook on the table and raised his eyebrows in concern.

"Did something happen today?"

Clémence blinked back. His warm brown eyes anchored her back to reality. "It was awful. Rachel, the girl I told you about? Nicole Blake's assistant? She's dead."

His jaw dropped. "What? Didn't you just meet her yesterday?"

She slowly nodded. "I was supposed to meet her again today. She hanged herself. We found her body in her hotel room."

She relayed the day's events, how Rachel had been M.I.A. until they convinced a hotel clerk to check her room, and how her body had been swinging from a chandelier.

"That must've been one sturdy chandelier," Arthur remarked.

Clémence looked up at their own crystal chandelier dangling over their heads in the salon. Everything was more fragile in Haussmanian buildings, and she was sure it wouldn't have been able to withstand the weight if anyone tried to hang themselves on her chandelier.

"But it's the Athena Hotel," Clémence said. "They completely renovated five years ago, gutted the place and put in modern appliances, new piping, and walls that were thick enough that you wouldn't hear the other guests. That chandelier was probably screwed in with industrial strength."

"True. So do you think Rachel committed suicide?"

"Well, the police are ruling it as a suicide. Her smartphone was on the coffee table, and she'd opened a notepad app and typed in, 'I can't go on anymore.'"

"So suicide is likely, then?" he asked.

Clémence sighed. "The wallpaper on her phone was set to a photo of Nicole Blake. When Rachel and I exchanged numbers yesterday, her wallpaper was definitely different. It was of cartoon frogs. I remember because I had thought it was weird and cute that she'd use that wallpaper. I think someone killed Rachel and tried to pass off her death as a suicide. The killer might've changed her phone's wallpaper to make it look as if Rachel was obsessed with Nicole, and wrote the message in Rachel's phone to make it sound like a suicide note. I don't know if this death was premeditated or not, but it's connected to Nicole's death."

"Hmm." Arthur took the glass from Clémence's firm clutch. She was gripping it so hard that it looked like the glass might break. He took a sip then asked, "Were there any witnesses at the time of her death? Perhaps hotel maids or other guests who might've heard something?"

"No. There was a Do Not Disturb sign on her door, so a maid probably hadn't been in since yesterday. I haven't heard from Rachel all morning. She was probably dead since last night. They're doing an autopsy right now, so we'll find out soon."

Arthur put his arm around Clémence's shoulders. "I'm sorry you had to see another dead body. Are you all right?"

"It's just revolting. My instincts tell me that Nicole was killed. Rachel was probably sniffing around, getting too close to the truth. Somebody staying in that hotel killed her, somebody on that film set, I'm sure of it."

Clémence rubbed her temples. A headache was forming. All these suspects and clues were clogging her head, and chaos reigned in her brain. Arthur knew her well enough to reach for her notebook and pen and pass them to her.

"Let's start from the beginning," he said. "Who's a suspect? Who's benefiting from Nicole's death?"

Clémence flipped to a fresh page. It reassured her to know that she'd solved cases before. She could do it again.

"Sarah Briar," she said. "I haven't met her yet, but she was losing her star power and sliding into supporting roles in the past couple of years. Sarah's supposedly nice, well, nicer than Nicole, but is it a coincidence that she's getting a meatier role in the film now that Nicole's gone? Plus, she'll get all the magazine covers to promote the film, and it might just lift her status back up to A-list."

"Where was she during Nicole and Rachel's deaths?" Arthur asked.

"I'm not sure yet. I've asked Sophie to help me get the film's shooting schedule. Sophie's sort of friends with Sarah, so she can also help me get a meeting with her. Sophie doesn't think it's Sarah, but she might be biased because of their new friendship."

"Do you really think that Sarah Briar, a petite blonde, can kill another human being so easily?"

"I did some research on her," Clémence said. "She did an action film five years ago, so she had training. She learned all sorts of martial arts, so I wouldn't underestimate her. It's possible, especially if she surprised Rachel or Nicole. Nicole was probably killed during the night, so what if she surprised her under some bridge along the Seine? And with Rachel, what if she had an extra key somehow and snuck into her room? The only thing that doesn't make sense is that she probably wasn't the person Nicole was secretly meeting."

"It is possible that Nicole just had a secret boyfriend or something," Arthur said.

"Yeah. And Sarah could've followed her one night. Who knows?"

"Okay. So who else do you suspect?"

Clémence was starting to get in the zone now that Arthur was here to keep her in line.

"Zach Brant. He didn't get along with Nicole on set for some reason. Was it a clashing of two big egos, or sexual tension? I haven't met him either, but their disdain for each other seems to be common knowledge among the crew. Sarah's going to be shooting all day tomorrow, and Zach's getting the day off, so Sophie's arranged it so I can go to the hotel and talk to Zach at the bar. My plan is to get him to talk, about anything at all. Something's gotta slip."

"So those are your two main suspects? Anyone else?"

"As a matter of fact, yes." Clémence brought up the director's wife, and told him about their encounter with her in Chris's suite. "Cynthia Collins, née Harper. She falls into the profile of the jealous wife. With all the beauty, money, and privilege in the world, she'd failed as an actress, and now she's a housewife. Her kids seem to like her, or at least respect her, but she seemed to be bored with her life, and even her own husband was afraid of her. You should've seen the way she looked at Sophie and me. If she could hate us, imagine how much she would've hated someone like Nicole, who basically grew up in a trailer park. Plus, her husband probably gushed about Nicole and her talent. She must've been green with envy."

"Could she have been cold-blooded enough to kill a young woman and toss her body into the river?" Arthur asked. "Then strangle another young woman to death? It's not as if she had any martial arts training either."

"I wouldn't rule it out," Clémence said. "She was about 5'8", and I'm sure running around a couple of young kids would require strength. Her look alone could kill."

Clémence wrote all her thoughts down. Then she reached into her black Alexander Wang purse, which was lying on the floor next to her couch, and pulled out Nicole's agenda. She flipped to the coded entries.

"I really need to crack the code and figure out who she was meeting. Who–or what–is OVUJOV? If I can crack one, I'll crack the others."

Arthur took a look through the agenda. "Why don't you try to figure out an easy one? Let's see, on the day before her death, there's nothing in her agenda except for her call time on set, and this meeting with OVUJOV. That doesn't help, but what if you try to decode one on a date when she had more appointments? Like this one, August fifteenth. She obviously had the day off. And isn't ILILIL one of the codes you were trying to crack?"

Clémence looked at her schedule. They listed stores around Rue Saint-Honoré. "Look, she went to Chateau du Chocolat. I doubt Sophie went with her. She says they didn't know each other at all. ILILIL has to be code for something, because I tried to look it up online and found nothing."

"What if it's a person?" Arthur said.

"It's a possibility. Maybe the decoded name would make more sense. But maybe you're on to something, because all these stores are around the Rue Saint-Honoré area. If ILILIL is a place, it could be around."

"It doesn't hurt to look around and keep your eyes peeled."

"You know what? After I speak to Zach Brant, I'll walk around Rue Saint-Honoré and see if there's anything that could give me a clue."

"She didn't do much that day, it seems, except shop in this area," Arthur added.

Miffy came in, tail wagging and with what looked like a smile on her face. She jumped up onto the couch and buried her face into Clémence's lap.

Clémence yawned. "Even Miffy's tired."

Arthur stood up. "Come on. You should rest early. I know you'll have a big day ahead of you."

Chapter 9

"You're going to meet Zach Brant?" Celine was so excited she was practically jumping up and down. "Can I come?"

Clémence hadn't realized Celine was behind them when she told Sebastien and Berenice in the kitchen who she was going to see that day.

"He's a murder suspect," Clémence said. "It's not a fan meet and greet."

"But maybe I can just hang back and just, you know, stare at him."

"I don't know if you'd be able to contain yourself," Sebastien quipped.

"He's actually right for once," Berenice said. "You're squealing at the mention of his name. No way would you be able to keep your cool once you see him again in the flesh."

Celine scowled. "Fine. You're probably right. I just love the man too much."

Sebastien gave her a dubious look. "Even though he might've killed Nicole Blake?"

Celine rolled her eyes. “It’s not him. He’s too handsome and talented to be capable of murder.”

“Isn’t one of your ex-boyfriends on trial for murder?” Berenice asked. “Wasn’t he handsome and talented as well?”

“Oh, he wasn’t my boyfriend,” Celine said. “We went out on one date, and that was it. I didn’t know him that well.”

“And you think you know Zach Brant?” Sebastien asked dryly.

“I do,” Celine said defensively.

“Aside from his favorite color and other useless facts, I mean.”

Celine put her hands on her hips. “I’m telling you, Zach wouldn’t do it. He’s a gentleman. He’s a kind person. On his last film, his stunt double broke a leg, and he visited him at the hospital all the time. Plus, whenever he breaks up with a girl, they stay on good terms. He’s the type of guy to treat the whole crew. I heard that he was the one who got his assistant to buy the cast and crew all the Damour stuff.”

“I don’t know if that’s true,” Berenice said. “Their catering crew buys the food.”

“The food, yes, but not necessarily gourmet desserts from Damour.”

"If he was such a nice guy, why didn't he get along with Nicole Blake?" Clémence asked.

"Oh, I don't know. Who does get along with Nicole Blake? She had a reputation for being difficult to work with."

"What if they were dating?"

"No," Celine said resolutely. "She's not his type."

"Why not?" Clémence asked.

"Zach has only gone out with brainy brunettes, based on his last two high-profile romances anyway. Personality-wise, Nicole's not Zach's type either. Nicole's a blonde in looks and in brain."

"What kind of guy doesn't like blond bomb-shells?" Berenice asked.

"Zach Brant," Celine replied with a tone of exas-peration. "He likes the girl-next-door type who's also smart. He said so in an interview once. Nicole's sexuality would've been too in his face. But there's always going to be rumors."

"I did read somewhere that Zach and Nicole were going out," Sebastien said.

The girls looked at him. Berenice was the most amused. "Where? *Closer* Magazine?"

"No, in *Le Parisien*," he replied.

"You shouldn't take it seriously," Celine said. "They were photographed a couple of times around Paris, but they could've just been rehearsing, or getting to know each other, since they were supposed to be playing lovers."

Celine pulled up some tabloid pictures on her phone. In one, they were at a restaurant, at a table. The photo was dim and fuzzy, but she could see that it was the two movie stars. Zach was leaning back in his chair with his arms crossed, and Nicole was leaning in, smiling. Zach's body language seemed defensive. It couldn't have been a date, could it?

"Maybe they had gone out, but they broke up," Berenice suggested. "And now they hate each other."

Sebastien shrugged. "Some people just don't get along in highly pressurized settings, especially when they have to work together twenty-four, seven. It's a miracle I've able to tolerate you guys for so long. So maybe the real reason was simple. Their personalities just didn't click. Isn't it obvious by the photo here? Zach obviously despises Nicole, and Nicole seems oblivious."

When Clémence got to the Athena Hotel, Sophie hadn't arrived yet. She'd texted Clémence to say that the director had called her to go on set at the last minute, but that Zach had confirmed that he'd be in the Blue Bar.

Without Sophie to introduce her, it would be more awkward to approach him, but then again, interrogating a murder suspect was never easy. Clémence took a deep breath and entered the bar. Even from afar, Zach made a strong impression. There were certain men whose beauty glowed as much as women's, and Zach was one of them. Dressed down in a gray V-neck tee and faded blue jeans, he was hunched over his table, drinking something on the rocks and reading his phone. At ten thirty in the morning, the bar was not busy, but the handful of patrons, women and men, kept darting glances over at the dirty-blond actor.

Clémence was surprised to find herself a bit intimidated by him. She wasn't a huge fan and thought his acting was on the bland side. Usually she found celebrities to be a bit of a disappointment when she met them in person, but she was surprised to find Zach to be even better looking in real life. His skin was tanned, bringing out the blue of his eyes. And with those muscular shoulders and forearms, he obviously spent time in the gym.

When she approached the bar, he looked up at her with alarm. Then his beautiful mouth turned upwards into a knowing smile. He probably thought she was a fan wanting an autograph.

"*Bonjour*, I'm Clémence."

Since he was American, she stuck out her hand, and he shook it. He gave her a lightning-quick once-over, but he didn't seem to be checking her out so much as sizing her up. Clémence spoke right away.

"I know you're here to meet Sophie, but she got called on set, and she told me to give you the message that she wasn't going to make it."

"Oh." Zach frowned, but nodded. "She said she wanted to speak to me about something important."

"I can fill you in. Do you mind if I join you?"

Zach looked reluctant. "Um. Sure."

"Actually, she called you here because I was the one who wanted to speak to you."

That knowing smile spread back onto his face. "Clémence, is it?"

"Yes."

"Look, I'm sure you're very nice, and you're very pretty, but I just got out of a breakup, and, well–"

Clémence was too stunned to laugh. "No, no. It's nothing like that. I'm not a fan."

"Oh." He looked surprised then slightly offended. "You're not?"

"No. Well. I mean, you're good in your movies and everything, but I'm not here on some, you know, romantic quest."

This was certainly getting awkward. She didn't know whether to laugh or cry out of embarrassment.

"I'm sure that you have lots of girls chasing after you," Clémence continued, "but I'm not one of them. Also, uh, I have a boyfriend."

Zach ran a hand through his hair. "God, I must've sounded arrogant."

"No, no, it's fine. I don't blame you for assuming that," Clémence reassured him.

"Sorry. Do you want something to drink? I know it's a little too early for alcohol."

"I'm fine. I just had a coffee. I'd like to ask you some questions about the recent deaths of Nicole and Rachel."

Zach examined her with new interest. "Are you a cop?"

"Well, no. But I do have some questions."

"I'm confused. They already questioned me a couple of days ago. Who are you?"

"I work with the police and help them with murder cases."

That was a bit of an exaggeration, considering that Inspector Cyril St. Clair couldn't stand her. But at least she had their respect, and if push came to shove, St. Clair would agree that she was working for them. They should really be paying her.

"Okay, but I thought you guys had already asked me everything. I was talking to that tall skinny guy for what felt like eternity. What else do you need to know?"

"Rachel Caufman, Nicole's assistant, died yesterday. Were you aware of that?"

"Yes, I did hear about that. It's very unfortunate that she would take her life like that."

Clémence blinked at him. She thought he could've sounded more concerned about her death, but if he couldn't emote well enough for the big screen, perhaps he was simply an inexpressive guy.

"Do you really think Rachel committed suicide?" she asked him.

He shrugged. "I don't know. I didn't really know Rachel too well, but she followed Nicole around like a puppy on set. It was her job, I supposed. I heard she killed herself because she was depressed that Nicole had died."

"And you think that's a plausible reason for Rachel to kill herself?" Clémence asked.

"Well, no, not for the average person, but Stockholm syndrome, right? I've experienced some weird things with fans. They can get a bit...crazy."

"Do you think Nicole was a likeable person?"

"Well, I didn't hate her, if that's what you mean." There was an edge of defensiveness in Zach's voice. Clémence was on the right track.

"That's not what I heard," she said.

He rubbed a hand over his lips.

"Look, it's true that we weren't exactly best friends, but–did you know Nicole?"

"No, but I'm trying to."

"If you didn't know her, you're lucky. She could be cruel, sadistic."

Clémence raised an eyebrow. "How so?"

"She liked to stir things up, cause drama, see people squirm."

"Did she make you squirm?"

"Sure. She made a lot of people squirm. Her favorite thing to do was to get people around her heated up, then sit back and watch the drama unfold."

"Is that what she did to you?"

"Tried to."

Clémence looked deeply into his bright blue eyes. "Did she have something on you?"

Zach blinked back. "What? No. She just didn't like me."

"Why not?"

"She didn't like a lot of people. She's only nice to people who could help her or benefit her in some way."

"But why not you? Sarah Briar, I could understand. They're competition. You're the leading man. As far as I've heard, Nicole's quite flirtatious with men."

He shook his head. "At first she was, but I could see through her act, and that's when she started hating me back. You either suck up to Nicole, like Rachel did, and get her approval, or you don't and get treated like dirt. I'm Zach Brant. I don't need some fake actress pushing me around."

His voice rose with passion as he spoke, causing the bartender to look their way.

"Then why do you have such chemistry on screen?" Clémence said.

"We're actors. It's what we get paid for."

"But don't you find Nicole attractive?" Clémence asked. "I mean, she was voted Maxim's hottest woman this year. Any hot-blooded male would find her attractive, right?"

Zach's eyes widened. Was there fear in his eyes? But why?

"Sure. Of course, she was beautiful. She was hot, even."

"So weren't you ever tempted to date her?"

"What does this have to do with the investigation?"

Clémence was firm. "Did you or did you not date?"

"Look, I can have my pick of hot girls. I do take personality into consideration, you know."

"What about Nicole? Are you saying she tried to seduce you and you didn't fall for it at all?"

"Would that be so hard to believe? Trust me, I didn't have a romantic relationship with Nicole. I did think she was interested, but I rejected her, and she took it badly. The atmosphere changed on set. She no longer spoke to me between takes."

Zach shrugged again and took the last chug of his drink. The ice rattled.

Clémence noticed a bruise on his forearm. Could it have come from a struggle with Rachel last night?

"What were you doing yesterday night?" Clémence asked.

"We were shooting, and I finished at about nine p.m. After that, I went home and crashed."

"Home as in here, in the hotel?"

"Yes." He looked at her, eyes squinting. "Am I a suspect for murder?"

Clémence did feel like he was hiding something. It wasn't what he said, but the way he said it. He was too defensive.

However, what he said was plausible. If Nicole did try to seduce him and her ego got bruised, it might've provoked her bad behavior.

When Clémence didn't answer, his voice rose in detectable fury. "You're kidding, right? Why would I murder Rachel, who I barely know?"

Clémence kept cool. The better she kept cool, the more Zach would unravel.

"Rachel was poking her nose around. She might've had a good idea who really murdered Nicole."

"And why in hell would you think I murdered Nicole?"

"What did Nicole have over you, Zach?"

His eyes dimmed. She thought she saw a glimmer of fear again, mixed with anger. She'd struck something.

"I told you," he said through gritted teeth. "She doesn't get along with a lot of people."

"I know she has something over you."

"You don't know what you're talking about." Not only did the bartender look their way again, but the other patrons as well.

"I'll find out," Clémence said in her low, cool voice.

"Are you done here?" Zach stood up and walked out of the Blue Bar without waiting for a response.

Chapter 10

Clémence talked a good talk, but she wasn't confident that she would find out what Zach hiding. And he was hiding something, because someone with nothing to hide wouldn't get angry and defensive so easily. The secret must've been something big.

Clémence took a cab to the Faubourg Saint-Honoré district. She got out and started walking down Rue Saint-Honoré. The neighborhood was the crème de la crème of design and fashion. During Paris Fashion week, all the fashionable jet-setters would descend in the area. She passed by Colette, Balenciaga, and Stuart Weitzman, as well as some high-end lingerie and perfume shops. She also passed by *Chateau du Chocolat*, where Nicole had visited, but where was ILILIL?

She passed the shoe store where Arthur bought his dress shoes in nearly every shade of brown, then she reached Place Vendome, where all the high-end jewelry shops were.

Maybe she was wasting her time looking for ILILIL. It seemed like a hopeless plan to be walking around aimlessly. Paris was massive. The neighborhood was big, and who was to say that Nicole didn't just hop in a cab and go to her secret meeting somewhere else?

Clémence wasn't exactly giving up, but she stopped looking so hard. Walking around Paris was her favorite thing to do anyway, and since she was already out and about, she might as well enjoy it.

She stopped in the Pierre Hermé on Avenue de l'Opéra to check out their latest macarons. A few tourists were outside the small shop, smiling for pictures as they posed with their macaron boxes. Tourists often did the same in front of the Damour patisseries.

Clémence chuckled and got in line. Sometimes she liked to see what the other patisseries were selling. Pierre Hermé was definitely their top competition when it came to macarons. Hermé was a family friend, and Clémence's parents called him the Picasso of macarons. He was Sebastien's hero.

She bought just one macaron in their newest flavor, Coffee, Orange Blossom & Candied Orange. Back out on the street, she took the macaron out of the plastic bag and took a bite. How did Hermé do it? The strange coffee and orange combination worked well, while the individual flavors burst in her mouth. She went back in and bought three more of the same flavor. Sebastien and Berenice needed to try them. Sebastien needed some inspiration from the competition to step up his macaron game.

Clémence considered what she should do next for the case since she was at a loss as to finding out what ILILIL was. She couldn't talk to Sarah Briar until the next day, when Sophie had arranged for her to meet her on set. She wanted to talk to Sarah today, but her schedule was packed. Not only was she shooting on set, she also had interviews and even a quick photoshoot in the 2nd arrondissement, which could go into the evening. And there was also Cynthia Collins to worry about. Who knew when she was going to show up on set. Perhaps she could ask Sophie if she could go on set after all in case Cynthia was there.

When she was about to whip out her phone to call Sophie, she noticed a store across the street. The sign was a mint green, with purple bubble letters forming the name Bébébé. She'd never heard of the store before.

When the cars on Avenue de l'Opéra came to a stop, she crossed the street. The window display featured a high-tech stroller and a minimalistic and modern transparent plastic crib. The store seemed to sell outrageously expensive products for babies. Could the store be the one Nicole Blake visited? ILILIL. BÉBÉBÉ. The syllables matched. A quiver of excitement shot through her as she pushed open the door.

"*Bonjour*," a redheaded saleswoman greeted her brightly. "Welcome to Bébébé."

"*Bonjour*," Clémence replied.

A few patrons were walking around the store, all women. Two were noticeably expecting.

"Are you looking for something in particular?" the saleswoman asked.

Clémence looked around. There were bath tubs, baby bottles, and towel sets. She'd never heard of the store before, but then again, she wasn't pregnant.

"Yes. I'm expecting."

She had blurted out the lie without thinking, and she immediately regretted it. What if the saleswoman recognized her as the Damour heiress? She'd be in the gossip blogs again.

The saleswoman didn't seem recognize Clémence, however. She seemed pleased to hear about the news.

"Really? How far along are you?"

"It's pretty, uh, new," Clémence answered. "Very new. And unexpected. But I'm pleased. I'm just, you know, browsing. How long has this store been here?"

"About four years. It has always done well, but ever since Prince George was photographed in one of our beanie hats, the brand has really taken off. We sell online as well."

"I heard about this place because of Nicole Blake," Clémence said. "She'd been in recently, hadn't she?"

The saleswomen looked conflicted about answering at first. "She was. I suppose word gets around. It's unfortunate what happened to her."

"Yes. Terrible."

"What a shame, because she was expecting too."

Clémence stared at her. "Really? She was pregnant?"

"I assumed. I was the one who'd helped her, but I didn't press her, of course. She wanted to see the products for girls, so maybe she was expecting a girl, or at least hoping for one. I can recognize a mother's glow, and she definitely had it."

"Wow."

"Yes, which makes the tragedy even more tragic. I was a big fan."

The saleswoman shook her head sadly.

"Me too," Clémence said.

So that was what Nicole had over Zach. She'd been pregnant with his daughter, a child that he didn't want.

Chapter 11

Clémence was tempted to buy some cute baby booties and a cashmere baby blanket from Bébébé, but she resisted since she wasn't actually having a baby, and she didn't want to freak Arthur out. They hadn't even talked about marriage yet, and frankly she wasn't sure she was even ready for the whole nine yards. She was quite in love with Arthur, but they'd only been going out for five months. There was no need to rush.

However, she was starting to get warm fuzzy feelings whenever she passed babies on the street and children in playgrounds. Their cute chubby cheeks, their dimpled fingers, their infectious laughter. Sometimes Clémence did have the urge to have a baby. Of course, she wasn't married yet. Not that a woman needed to be married to have a child, but it would be nice.

Nicole Blake wasn't married when she got pregnant. That is, if what the saleswoman said was true. Was the father Zach? And did he murder her because she was pregnant? Whether it was true or not, the whole situation was sad.

Rachel must've not known about Nicole's pregnancy. If she did, she would've mentioned it.

Clémence had read all the recent tabloid articles about Nicole Blake, and there was a rumor that she'd dated a man named Elon Marchese. Elon was a French businessman who owned a few luxury fashion companies. He didn't work in the film industry, which would've made it easier for them to keep the relationship a secret if he and Nicole had been an item. Their relationship was never confirmed officially. There was only speculation in the media that came from anonymous sources. Clémence didn't know how reliable that was.

The only proof she'd seen was a blurry photograph taken of them, presumably on a guest's phone, at a charity event. They were only talking, but the source in the article claimed that they were hanging on to each other's every word throughout the evening, and they got together because they bonded over their love of fashion. Elon was in his mid-forties. He was handsome and rich. Clémence could see the appeal. Whether the rumors were true or not was another story, but she made a mental note to investigate further into their relationship.

She hailed a cab back to her apartment in the 16th arrondissement. Miffy jumped on her as soon as she entered the apartment.

"I missed you too, girl." Clémence kissed her then went into the kitchen to pour dog food in her dish.

She hadn't heard from Cyril about the autopsies, but it wasn't as if he'd always been forthcoming with information. He only agreed to work with her when he was stumped, and he was stumped often. However, his ego was big, so he wouldn't ask for help. He was probably all too happy when Clémence helped, even if he would never admit it in a million years.

"Cyril," she said when he picked up. "What's the news?"

She could practically hear him roll his eyes on the other line. He sighed and resigned himself to telling her. "Rachel was strangled, and not by the belt around her neck. There were bruises on her neck, and in other areas on her body."

"So I was right," Clémence said. "She was murdered."

"Yes, fine," he said with exasperation. "She was. We did find traces of DNA around the room, but they could be from a number of people. The maids, guests she'd invited into the house, or even past guests. We're in the middle of sorting that out right now."

"What about Nicole Blake?" Clémence said.

"What about her? I already told you the results. Her head had injuries, but she could've hit her head on rocks and such in the river."

"You didn't do a full autopsy, did you? I mean, did you know that she was pregnant?"

Clémence wasn't completely sure, but she had to sound certain.

"Pregnant?" Cyril exclaimed. "Where did you get that?"

"Do the autopsy and make sure. Call me back to confirm once you've done so."

She hung up. Cyril was probably fuming, but no doubt he'd take her tip and do as she said. He had no choice because he was stumped.

She noticed that she'd received a text message from Ben asking her if he could come down to her place to do his laundry. The apartment that Clémence was living in actually belonged to her parents. They were in Asia for a few months, overseeing the operations of their new patisseries in Tokyo, Hong Kong, and now Singapore.

They'd rented their *chambre de bonne* to Ben. Ever since Clémence had introduced him to Berenice, they'd been a couple. Clémence had also become close friends with Ben, especially since he came over to do his laundry every week.

From his room on the top floor, he could see into Clémence's kitchen, so he'd probably seen that she was home. After she texted back that he could, he knocked on the kitchen door in no time.

"*Coucou*," Clémence greeted him.

Lanky, dark-haired, pale-skinned Ben was always dressed in black. He was a writer and Clémence assumed that was his writer's uniform.

"How are you?" He grinned. There was a mischievous quality about him when he smiled.

"Oh, not much, just starting to make a late lunch. You hungry?"

"I just ate, thanks." He'd dragged in his linen laundry bag, and he started using the washing machine in the kitchen.

Clémence got along with Ben because they were both artists at heart. Ben hung out with a lot of artists, writers, and musicians in Paris, and he was always pushing her to finish her paintings so she could put on a show.

"I know what you're going to ask," Clémence said. "No, I haven't finished my paintings yet."

"Actually, I was going to ask how the murder case is going."

"Oh, I guess Berenice told you about that?"

He nodded as he added detergent to the slot in the washing machine. "I'm a big fan of Nicole Blake. She kicked ass in Red Sniper."

"I didn't see that," Clémence said. "I forgot that she was in an action film. She was quite versatile, wasn't she?"

"She could play anything. Any leads on who killed her?"

"A few." Clémence gave him the rundown, and then she showed him Nicole's red agenda and explained how certain events were coded to protect her privacy.

"I didn't know she was so private," Ben said. "But I suppose she does have that aura of mystery about her that's so captivating on screen. Did you break the code?"

"I was about to start working on it." She continued to explain that she'd found out that Nicole had been in the baby store Bébébé. In the agenda, it had been coded as ILILIL. "As soon as I figure out how to decode it, I can decode the others."

"I bet it's a cipher," Ben said. "I use ciphers in the mystery novel I'm working on. Wait here."

He dashed upstairs. When he came back to the kitchen, he held out a round piece of paper.

Clémence took it. "This is the cipher?"

"Yup. It's easy to use."

It was basically two sets of alphabets, one lining around the bigger wheel and the other around the smaller one. She could spin the smaller wheel around for the letters to line up. She lined the "I" from ILILIL up with the "B" from Bébébé. It worked. The "L" lined up with "E."

She beamed at Ben. "This is it. This is the combination! Now I can crack OVUJOV. This is nerve-racking, because it could reveal the killer."

"This is so exciting." Ben leaned in over her shoulder as she wrote down the letters as she decoded them.

"H-O-N-C-H-O." Clémence frowned. "Honcho? Who or what could that be?"

"Maybe it's a nickname for someone."

"Another code?" Clémence sighed. "Honcho...it does sound male."

"You have someone in mind, don't you?"

"I think it's Zach Brant. There was something between him and Nicole. I couldn't tell whether it was love or hate. Now I find out Nicole was pregnant when she died. Maybe it was his child, and he killed her."

"I never liked Zach Brant," Ben said. "Something about his face. He's too good looking. And his acting is total crap. Was he going out with Nicole? I did hear they didn't get along."

"Apparently they didn't, but they made a convincing couple on screen. Their scenes together were supposed to be electric. When I interrogated Zach, he said that Nicole tried to seduce him and he rejected her."

"Who doesn't like Nicole Blake?"

"That's what I said. But he hated her personality. He basically said she was manipulative and fake. Even Rachel said this was true about her."

"So Nicole Blake's not perfect. Even if she was pregnant with his child, would it be so bad for him? His star power would rise."

"Zach is only twenty-five. I doubt he'd want to be a father at such a young age, especially when he's got the world at his feet. Maybe he felt as if he was tricked into sleeping with her. Knowing her, she might've threatened him with going public, and he made a rash decision and killed her to silence her. I mean, with that temper of his, it's plausible."

"Maybe," Ben said, but he didn't seem convinced. "Lots of men get women pregnant accidentally. In this case, however, he had more to gain if Nicole was pregnant. It's not like he would have to marry her. Even if he did, they would've been a power couple; their careers would've skyrocketed."

"Okay, maybe you're right. But there's also this Elon guy." Clémence told Ben about Nicole's other rumored boyfriend. "What if Nicole was really pregnant with Elon's baby, and Zach was jealous? What if he was really in love with her? He was very passionate when he spoke about Nicole. Love could easily cross over to hate."

"Maybe," Ben said.

Clémence stood up and paced. "So Zach might've killed her because she was having Elon's baby. Or Elon might've killed Nicole because she was having Zach's baby."

Chapter 12

Carolyn, Damour's head manager, had gone home sick. Celine called Clémence to come in because they needed help at the *salon de thé.* They were dealing well with the heavy traffic at the restaurant until a customer became upset about a lost reservation and demanded to see a manager. Since Damour was less than a five-minute walk from her apartment, Clémence agreed to come in and sort it out.

After talking to the irate man, she could tell that he was lying and never made a reservation in the first place. Bad liars usually had a tell, and he blinked too much when he was insistent on his story that he'd made the reservation five days ago. Clémence didn't want to reward liars, but luckily for him, a table opened up by the time he'd finished ranting, and Clémence showed him and his wife to their seats. She would keep a closer eye on this couple in the future.

Since she was already at Damour, she decided to check in the kitchen. When she entered, the sweet aromas hit her. She never got tired of the smell of a kitchen, especially one that was as big and busy as the one at Damour. The energy and rhythm of her bakers and chefs never failed to liven her up. She went to her usual spot at Berenice and Sebastien's table. A tray of lavender madeleines had just come out of the oven. Sebastien was mixing the lemon glaze to dip them in, but Clémence couldn't help trying one. It was a new flavor that she hadn't tried after all.

"Delish," Clémence said.

The madeleines recalled what Rachel said about how much Nicole Blake loved Damour madeleines. She would've loved the lavender ones.

"What happened to Carolyn anyway?" Clémence asked.

"I don't know," Berenice answered. "She'd been nauseous all morning. It might be food poisoning, since she dined out with her husband at some new restaurant last night."

"I hope she's alright."

Clémence shot Carolyn a text, asking how she was.

"Clémence, are we still on to work on the new éclair flavors for our winter collection? I have some ideas."

"Oh, sorry, Sebastien. I know I said I would, but I have to do something tomorrow."

"Clémence is in the middle of a murder case, remember?" Berenice said. "You know how she gets when she's investigating."

"Oh yeah. I forgot," Sebastien said sheepishly. "How's that going?"

Before she could answer, Clémence got a call on her cell phone. It was her friend, fashion designer Marcus Savin.

"Clémence, *ma belle*," the top designer greeted her in his jovial voice when she answered.

"*Ça va*, Marcus? Are you all ready for fashion week?"

"I live for fashion week in Paris," Marcus said. "You'll be getting an invite to my show soon, like I promised. Say you'll be there?"

"Of course I will." As long as she solved this murder case by then, that was.

"Great. I have you seated in the front row. Sophie and Madeleine Seydoux are both walking in my show. Are you sure you don't want to walk too?"

"*Non*, Marcus. I really wouldn't be good on the runway. I'd probably fall, and people will probably put that up on YouTube. Plus, I'm too short to be a model."

"Come on, Clémence. Sophie is only five-foot-seven."

"Kate Moss is also five-seven. I'm only five-four. Trust me, I'm better behind the camera."

Marcus sighed. "I figured you'd say that, but you can't blame a poor designer for trying. So here's the thing. You know how my ready-to-wear collection is inspired by Damour's desserts?"

"Yes." Marcus had consulted her about his collection. She'd given him a lot of free macarons and other colorful treats to inspire him. As a result, many of his pieces were in the vibrant shades of Damour macarons. The fabrics used were as light as the cream of their pastries and cakes.

"I just had the fabulous idea of incorporating real desserts in the show. They need to be eye-catching, so I'm thinking cakes. Big, extravagant cakes to match the outfits."

"How extravagant?" Clémence asked.

"Enough to make a statement, but not too much to take the attention away from the clothes. The cake and the clothes should complement each other. I'm thinking one cake could be dotted with macarons. Another can be a multi-tiered opéra cake. And then a Charlotte Royale cake. All with a Damour twist."

"Okay. I can visualize it. If I make an opera cake, that would match one of the coats in your collection. And the swirl pattern in your tops and skirts would go with the Charlotte Royale."

"*Exactement.* I knew you'd get it. You think that your bakers can do it for me in time?"

"Sure. The only problem is, the cakes can get pretty heavy. Are you sure these models can carry so much weight as they're walking down the runway?"

"That's true," Marcus said. "Well, they don't have to be real cakes. They just have to look like it."

"Okay, we'll use styrofoam on the inside. How's that?"

"Genius."

"Too bad you won't be able to eat them after."

"That's true."

"I'd be happy to make you an edible cake too, to celebrate the show."

"That'd be great, Clémence. Why don't you come in my studio on Friday, and we can discuss everything in person."

"Friday?" Clémence wasn't so sure that she could make it. What if she had to follow up on a lead? "Can I get back to you on that, Marcus?"

"Sure. But don't wait too long. Fashion week is three weeks away."

"We'll get it done, I promise."

"I'm so excited. It's a win-win for the both of us. Damour will surely get more publicity after the show."

"It sounds great, Marcus. Thanks for the opportunity. Hey, now that I have you on the phone, I want to ask, do you know anything about Nicole Blake?"

"Nicole? No. It's so sad, her death. I hadn't had the pleasure of meeting her, but I'd always wanted to. Now it's too late."

"Have you met Sarah Briar?"

"She's cute too. But no, haven't met her either."

"What about Zach Brant?"

"Zach?" His voice dropped. "Yes. We've dressed him once for the Venice Film Festival."

"What did you think of him?"

"Oh, you know, handsome as a goon." Marcus sounded resentful.

"Is that a bad thing?" Clémence asked.

"It is if the guy's trying to hit on your boyfriend."

"Wait, Zach was trying to hit on Brice?"

"Yes. You've met him. You know how gorg my Brice is. Zach Brant noticed it too. This was three years ago, when Zach wasn't as famous. When we were doing the fitting one day, Brice came in, and Zach spent the whole time buttering him up."

"What are you saying? Zach is gay?"

"Yes. Of course he's gay. I'm surprised no one has caught on."

"Fully gay?"

"Well, who knows, but you've seen the girls he's dated. Total snoozers. You'd be surprised how many seemingly straight guys are gay in the film business."

"Wow."

"I'm surprised there haven't been more gay rumors about Zach," Marcus said.

"Are you sure?" Clémence asked.

"I didn't ask him outright, but I know when someone's trying to hit on my boyfriend. It was very disrespectful, and now I'm never going to dress the guy again."

"Oh boy," Clémence said. "My friend Celine is going to be disappointed to find out about this."

Chapter 13

The film crew was shooting in a house in Montmartre. When Clémence reached the small winding streets north of Paris, she spotted the house Sophie had texted her the address of.

Sophie was shooting that morning. She had a scene with Zach Brant, who was playing her boyfriend. Since films were shot out of sequence, this was a scene from the beginning of the film, before Zach's character dumped Sophie for Nicole.

Sarah Briar was also supposed to be on set later that morning. The schedule gave Clémence an opportunity to talk to Zach first.

In a white house with vines crawling up one side, sectioned off from the street by a gated brick wall, crew members were coming and going out of the front door. The house across the street, which was similar but pink, was where the actors were shooting. Clémence could see the lights set up inside through the windows. There were also wires coming out the front door that were connected to power generators.

She arrived early in the morning at eight a.m. as Sophie had suggested. The call time for the actors had been earlier, at six thirty a.m., and they should've been finished with their makeup and wardrobe by now. As she walked through the front gate, a young woman holding a clipboard and wearing a headset stopped her. She looked straight out of a '90s American grunge music video in her red flannel shirt and ripped jeans. Clémence told her that she'd been invited by Sophie Seydoux.

"Right." The girl inspected her with her coal-rimmed eyes. Her nose ring glistened in the sunlight. "Sophie did tell me she was expecting you. But you're not a reporter, are you?"

Clémence was dressed in a more subdued outfit—a black V-neck sweater, gray tweed pants, and black ballerina Chanel flats. She wondered what part of her outfit screamed reporter, but perhaps the girl had gotten used to reporters coming on set to interview the actors.

"Ah, no. I'm just a friend."

"Are you here for a reason?"

"Well, I'm looking for a change in career. I'm considering working on film sets, so Sophie invited me to come and check it out."

"Oh? What fields are you interested in?"

"I don't know. Maybe costume design?"

"Sophie might be able to introduce you to Breanne Dune. She's our costume designer."

"Okay, sure. Thanks."

"Sophie's on the second floor, second room to the left, in the room marked with her name."

"Thanks. What's your name?"

"Jane."

"Thanks, Jane."

Clémence went upstairs, passing a couple of sleepy-looking crew members on the way. Sophie's door was closed, and she was about to knock when she noticed Zach's name on the door next to hers. His door was ajar, and Clémence peeked in.

Oddly enough, Zach was snacking on some madeleines. Clémence wondered if they were from Damour. It was; she spotted Damour's signature lavender bag embossed with their gold logo on a coffee table. She supposed the crew was still getting their desserts and snacks from Damour even now that they'd moved to Montmartre.

"Clémence?" Zach opened the door wider.

She jumped back. How could he have seen her? Then she saw the full-length mirror against the back wall. He'd probably seen her reflection.

"*Bonjour*," Clémence said awkwardly.

Zach's beautiful features were already twisted into a look of annoyance. "What are you doing? Are you even allowed to be here?"

"I was visiting Sophie."

"Sure you are. Are you here to accuse me of murder again, or were you hoping to catch me without a shirt on?"

Clémence rolled her eyes. She entered his room without being asked in and shut the door behind her. "Zach, remember when I said I was going to figure out what you were hiding? I know what your secret is."

"What? How I was sneaking off on trysts with Nicole, that I couldn't possibly resist her?"

He was trying to sound full of bravado, but his smile had faltered, and Clémence could detect a hint of worry in his eyes.

"I know you're gay."

His blue eyes flashed with surprise, but he quickly recovered, twisting his lips into an even meaner smirk. "What? That's the best you've got?"

"Come on, you're gay. I know you are." Clémence crossed her arms and tilted her head at him expectantly.

"Please. Every actor's the subject of gay rumors."

"You're from a small town in Texas. Growing up, you had to prove your masculinity, didn't you?

Is that why you've never gotten along with your father? I read your interviews. He used to be a star quarterback in high school, and all you wanted to do was go to theatre class."

"That's not true," Zach insisted. Blood rose to his cheeks. For an actor, he wasn't good at hiding his feelings.

"Did he use to beat you?" Clémence asked softly.

Zach got more and more red.

"What's the shame in being gay?" Clémence tried again. "What did your father do to you?"

"He was a bastard," Zach growled. "He did beat me, but it was because he was a bastard. Not because I was gay."

"And your mother," Clémence continued, "she's a devout Catholic. She must've cried herself to sleep knowing you are who you are. That's why you moved so far away. That's why you're not speaking to them anymore, even though you've made millions at the box office."

"You don't know anything about my mother. For the last time, I'm not gay!"

"And I heard you turned down the starring role in the Harvey Milk biopic. Why was that?"

"The script was awful. I didn't get along with the director."

"The film won two Academy Awards," Clémence said.

He looked as if he either wanted to punch something or break down and cry.

"Give it up, Zach," Clémence said softly. "Keeping this secret is eating you up inside, isn't it? Always having to act macho, taking on the role of the handsome love interest, or the asshole frat boy, or the infallible action hero. I know you're an actor, but you can't pretend to be someone else in real life too."

Zach sat down on his sofa. His eyes fluttered, and he looked as if he wanted to disappear. "Yes," he whispered. "Okay. Fine. You got it. I'm...I'm attracted to men."

"Nicole knew, didn't she?"

"Yes. She found out. But I wasn't lying when I said that Nicole tried to seduce me. First day on set here in Paris, she called me into her hotel room to practice my lines with her. When I came in, she was on her bed, completely naked."

"So she knew then, when you rejected her?"

"Maybe. She watched me closely after that. I guess her ego was bruised. And I was also in a relationship with someone, a stunt devil, and I guess she found out that I was always contacting him to see if he was alright when he was in the hospital after a stunt gone wrong. And there are some attractive grips on set. She must've caught me admiring them on occasion. It was my own fault for not being more careful. She knew. And she tortured me about it, always threatening that she'd go to the press about it one day, or she'd just let something slip by accident. I really hated her. She just loved seeing me squirm."

Zach was gripping a water bottle that he'd picked up from the coffee table. The veins of his bicep muscles popped. He threw the bottle against the wall.

Clémence flinched, but Zach only buried his head in his hands. "My career would've been ruined. God, did she enjoy seeing me suffer. Every day, she'd taunt me. She'd put pages from gay magazines under my door, or prompt the guys to make gay jokes whenever we were standing around on set, knowing that this would all hurt me."

"Do you actually think she would've revealed your secret?"

"Yes, if I'd pissed her off enough. But she would've wanted to hold on to the secret for as long as possible. She loved having control over others." Zach rubbed his face, hard. "So what, now that you know, are *you* going to out me? Tell the police that I killed Nicole because she had something against me?"

Clémence took a deep breath. "No."

Zach jerked his head back up at her in surprise.

"Because I don't believe you killed Nicole," Clémence said.

"You don't?"

"No. I think that as difficult as this was, you wouldn't kill over it. If your secret was revealed, isn't there a part of you that would've actually been relieved?"

Zach shook his head, but his body went limp. A softness came over his face. He let out a long sigh.

"Probably."

He looked up at Clémence, those famous blue eyes wounded. She could see the scared puppy behind that masculine facade.

"What would happen if you were to come out?" she asked.

"My life would change. Fans might abandon me. I wouldn't be getting the same job offers."

"Are those roles what you really want?"

His face scrunched up. Slowly, he shook his head. "I don't know. I'm starting to feel burnt out. My life is more truthful on film. I feel more real when I'm acting."

"Look, I'm not here to tell you what you should or shouldn't do with your career or your life," Clémence said. "It's not really my place. But if you're willing to risk being suspected of murder just to keep your secret, you're killing yourself on the inside."

"You're right. I hate to say it, but you are right. Enough people know my secret. They've been respectful not to reveal it, but I'm tired of the charade and the media games."

"Right now, you have bigger things to worry about. Someone on this set is a murderer."

"Are you sure?" Zach asked. "I always assumed she killed herself, and that you guys would come to that realization sooner or later. Take it from me. Some of us are really messed up. Who's to say that Nicole wasn't messed up enough to kill herself? She did all sorts of things for attention. Manipulating people, using her looks. The whole reason for her drive for fame was to be seen as someone superior, beautiful, talented, powerful. It wasn't enough, obviously. Maybe she realized that in the end."

"It does sound logical, but her assistant was definitely murdered."

Zach frowned. "Really?"

"Yes. The police confirmed it. Rachel was strangled by someone before being strung up to the chandelier with a belt. She knew too much. She was convinced that Nicole was murdered, and the day before her death, she was determined that I help her find out the truth."

"There were no fingerprints or DNA or anything?" Zach asked.

She shook her head. "They're working on it right now. And I'm here on this set doing my part. I need your help. You see, we also confirmed that Nicole had been pregnant when she died. The police just confirmed it this morning. Do you have any idea who could've gotten her pregnant?"

"What? No. I have no idea."

"You don't know if she had a boyfriend, or was seeing someone on set?"

"No. Nicole would never let anyone in on her private life. If Rachel didn't know, I would know even less. She'd do everything to uncover your secrets, but she would never reveal her own hand on purpose."

Clémence also told him about the agenda and the code name she had uncovered, Honcho.

"Honcho?" Zach repeated. "No, I've never heard that name."

"I've read in the papers that she might've been seeing someone named Elon Marchese. Do you know who he is?"

"Who's Elon? Elon...Elon...His name does sound familiar."

"He's a French businessman, and he has property in Paris, Miami, and L.A. He owns a few fashion houses–"

"Oh! I do know him. I've met him at parties and talked to him once. He's quite intimidating." Zach got quiet for a second. "You know, I do remember seeing him at the Athena Hotel a couple of weeks ago."

"Really? So he was dating Nicole?"

"No," Zach said. "I didn't see him coming out of Nicole's room. Sarah's room is right next to mine. We're both at one end of the hall. Once, I was coming out of my room and saw him walking past me. He'd been coming from the direction of Sarah's room."

"Are you sure it was him?"

"Yes, I saw his profile. He didn't see me though. He just got onto the elevator as I was coming up behind him."

"So Elon wasn't dating Nicole, but Sarah?"

"Maybe. I didn't think much of it at the time. Sarah's love life is none of my business. But yeah, maybe she is dating Elon."

"That explains it," Clémence said.

"Explains what?"

"Why Nicole and Sarah never got along. They were fighting over this guy."

What if Sarah killed Nicole because she found out that Elon had been cheating on her with Nicole? Clémence wouldn't put it past Nicole to taunt Sarah with her pregnancy.

Chapter 14

"*Salut*, Clémence." Sophie opened the door and greeted her with air kisses. Since her face was already fully made up, she made sure their cheeks didn't touch.

"You look adorable," Clémence said.

Her friend had always been famous, but she was excited that Sophie was on her way to becoming a movie star. While Sophie had acted in small roles in French films before, this was her first Hollywood production. She was wearing a striped boat shirt, and with her pixie cut, she reminded Clémence of Jean Seberg in Goddard's *À Bout de Soufflé*, another one of Clémence's favorite films.

"I'm nervous," Sophie said. "In the scene I'm shooting now, I have to cry on cue because Zach's character breaks up with me."

"I'm sure you'll be fine."

"What if the tears don't come?"

"Just think of your worst heartbreak and double it. If that doesn't work, just pinch yourself until the tears come."

Sophie laughed. “Thanks. Have you talked to any of your suspects yet?”

“I just spoke to Zach.”

“And?”

“He’s innocent.”

“Phew. That’s a relief, since I’m about to work with him. How’d you know?”

“It’s a long story,” Clémence said. Zach’s secret wasn’t hers to tell. “But I think it might actually be Sarah Briar. Or her boyfriend.”

“Why?”

“Did you know that she was dating Elon Marchese?”

“No. I knew she was seeing someone, but she never said who.”

“I think Nicole was dating Elon too. Nicole was also pregnant, possibly with his child.”

“What?” Sophie exclaimed.

“It’s a theory. Either Sarah or Elon might’ve had something to do with Nicole’s death.”

“I don’t know,” Sophie said. “Sarah’s so sweet. I don’t know if she’s the type that’s capable of murder.”

“After my experiences, a murderer can be any age, sex, and be from any social class. It really has to do with motive. Sarah has a motive. She had a lot to gain. Jealousy and passion could've been at play. If she's in love with Elon, she might have wanted to kill whoever stood in the way. And if Nicole took everything she wanted from her—acting jobs, the man, and now the baby—she might've wanted to do everything she could to keep what she could."

Sophie thought about it. "I guess I can see how her life has improved since Nicole has...gone. Sarah's getting a lot more attention in the press, but you can say the same about me. Wouldn't I be a suspect as well?"

Clémence smiled. "You're too cute to be a murderer."

"I know."

"Try to keep your eyes peeled, but I do want to talk to Sarah this afternoon."

Jane, the grunge girl Clémence met earlier, knocked on Sophie's door.

"Sophie? They want you on set."

"Thanks," Sophie replied. She looked back at her script and heaved a sigh. "I've never acted in English before, either. In the other scenes, I barely had any lines. Not that I'm complaining."

"You'll be fine," Clémence insisted.

"What are you going to do? It's a closed set right now, so I can't even get you in. If you offend her with all the murder questions, she might complain and get you thrown off set. She's nice, but she does have boundaries."

"The police probably questioned her already. I don't think telling her that I work for the police would help matters. Maybe you can just tell her I'm one of your friends and that I'm just visiting you on set. I already told Jane that I'm here to check out the film set because I'm thinking of a change in careers. Maybe that'll get her talking about the set. Plus, actors love talking about themselves, right? She might reveal more if I make her feel comfortable."

"Okay," Sophie said. "I really hope you're wrong, though. I like her."

Clémence thought that Sophie was too trusting. She wore her heart on her sleeve. This had resulted in her getting kidnapped after falling for a con artist in a whirlwind romance. If Sophie wanted to work in Hollywood, she would have to be more discerning.

"You can't come into the house we're shooting in right now," Sophie said, "but we're shooting in a café nearby this afternoon. Why don't you come back then? There's bound to be a lot of sitting around and waiting between setups, and I'm sure Sarah will be bored and will want to talk to you. She's usually quite chatty and friendly with the hair and makeup people, so I don't see why she wouldn't want to talk to you."

With nothing much else to do, Clémence took the Métro back to the 16th. After feeding Miffy, she took her iPad with her to the Damour kitchen. She wasn't there to work. She just liked spending time there because it was a place where she felt safe, especially when there was a murderer on the loose.

"You're still not ready to make the éclairs, are you?" Sebastien asked when she came in.

Berenice was on her break, and Sebastien was taking up the whole table with all the macarons he was making. The colorful shells were drying on trays before being put in the oven. He was making the ganache filling as he waited.

Clémence remembered that Marcus Savin wanted them to make cakes for his fashion show, and she told Sebastien.

"Really?" Sebastien broke out into a toothy smile. It was rare that he smiled–he was so serious–but when he did, it was like sunshine breaking through gray clouds.

"He wants me to go to his studio to see his designs and plan the cakes to complement them. Wanna come with me?"

"Sure. When?"

"As soon as I crack this murder case. Oh, it's not Zach Brant, by the way."

"Celine will be relieved."

Not when she finds out that he's gay, Clémence thought, but she kept quiet. Instead she brought up Elon Marchese. She looked him up on the internet to find out more about him.

"Get this, his company rivals LMVH. He's a pretty big deal. Not that handsome, but I can see the appeal. I wonder if Marcus knows whether he's in town right now."

"Call him," Sebastien said.

Clémence did just that, but she got his voicemail. She left a message asking him to call her back.

Chapter 15

At three p.m., Clémence left Damour to take a taxi back to Montmartre. When she passed the window display of the Damour patisserie, she saw a couple of kids pressing their noses against the glass at the colorful treats inside. The sight of their cute, delighted faces made her smile to herself. She remembered when she was a little girl spending time with her parents as they baked, watching in wonder at all the work that went into a delicious dessert. Now at the age of twenty-nine, she still wasn't sick of sweets and French pastries. Within the hour, she'd eaten a pistachio éclair, two pumpkin spice macarons, a *pain au chocolat*, and a *viennoise* to go with her coffee.

With a full stomach, she hailed a cab at Place du Trocadero to take her north of the city. Sophie had texted her the address of the café, which was away from the touristic part of Montmartre. On winding cobblestone roads, she passed the charming houses and buildings that were quainter than those in the rest of Paris. The production crew had blocked off the street to shoot in the café. Sophie was doing a scene where Sarah's character breaks it to Sophie that her boyfriend was two-timing Sophie with Nicole's character.

A small crowd had formed to watch the film shoot on the other side of the gated bar. Clémence waved to Jane, who recognized her and let her in.

Chris, the happy-go-lucky director, was standing next to his director's chair, talking to an assistant. He looked up and noticed Clémence.

"Clémence, right? What are you doing here?"

"Hi, Chris." She smiled. "Sophie said I could come by and observe the set. Hope that's all right."

"Sure, that's no problem." He leaned in and whispered, "Watch out for any serial killers among my crew." Then he laughed as if he'd made the funniest joke in the world.

Clémence politely smiled back.

"One of our extras called in sick," Chris continued. "I know you don't want to act, but how about filling in as an extra in this café scene?"

Out of the corner of her eye, she noticed Cynthia Collins standing around. In a black wool dress, she blended in with the shadows of the trees on the street. She was scowling in Clémence's direction.

Clémence was about to decline, but something about the way Cynthia was staring at her made her change her mind.

"Sure," she told Chris while holding Cynthia's gaze. "What do I have to do?"

"See the other extras in the café?"

Clémence turned around. There was a bartender, two businessmen at a table, and a middle-aged couple. It was silly, but Clémence had assumed the bartender was real, and the others were actual customers.

"All you have to do is drink a cup of coffee and read a newspaper," Chris said.

"I can do that," Clémence said.

"Good. What you're wearing is fine. Your hair looks good. Diane here will just put a bit of makeup on you, then off you go."

The makeup girl came up and started applying all sorts of powders and pencils on her. Clémence never felt comfortable in front of the cameras, but since extras were basically background scenery, it was fine. Besides, she'd be able to pick herself out on the big screen later on.

Sophie and Sarah were not on set yet when Clémence sat down at her designated table in the café. They arrived a few minutes later in a minivan, having already changed into their wardrobe, and had their hair and makeup done back in the white house that served as a green room. Chris greeted them and talked to them about their motivation for the scene. The makeup girl and a hairstylist did some touch-ups on the girls, then they were ready.

"*Bonjour.*" Sophie waved to Clémence and then turned back to Sarah. "This is my friend Clémence. Clémence, Sarah."

Clémence shook her hand. "I was just visiting Sophie on set, but ended up with a plum role as a coffee-drinking extra," she joked.

Sarah laughed graciously. Like Nicole Blake, she was also a stunning blonde, but there was something more homely about her, less bombshell. Her eyes were smaller, her lips thinner, but there was something charming about her all the same. She had a great smile, and her skin was luminous, the kind that lit up the silver screen. Could the beautiful actress really be a killer?

Clémence reminded herself not to get sucked in by appearances. The movie industry was all smoke and mirrors, and so was reality.

"Are you an actress?" Sarah asked Clémence in a perky voice, the friendly smile still on her face.

"Oh, I'm a horrible actress. No aspirations there."

"Sarah," Chris called. "I want you sitting here." As she sat where he wanted, he turned back to a crew member. "Can you bounce the light from this side of her face? Let's do a light test."

"How long do you think you'll be shooting for?" Clémence asked Sophie.

She shrugged. "Depends. He's pretty meticulous, so we could be doing take after take. Unless it's one of those rare days when he loves everything that we do and we can all just call it a day after two takes. I doubt it though. This is a bit of an emotional scene too. Fingers crossed that I nail it."

"Break a leg."

The actors took their places. They ran through the scene once before the director began rolling.

"Light? Camera. Action!"

Clémence read the most recent story about the French president's love life in the newspaper. He'd left his long-term girlfriend for a French movie star. The ex had just released a tell-all memoir about her time with the president, and it had caused a national scandal. Clémence didn't understand what it was about him that made these beautiful, intelligent women fight over him. She supposed power was a strong aphrodisiac. In any case, the president's love life was dramatic enough to deserve a movie of its own.

After seven takes, Clémence was starting to get bored. She was reading the same newspaper articles over and over again. How did these actresses maintain their energy levels to do a great job in every take? Clémence realized she had it easy, reading *Le Monde* and fake-drinking espresso.

On the fifteenth take, the director was finally happy. He wanted to shoot close-ups of the same scene immediately, which meant the actresses had to say the same lines again.

Clémence had always imagined movie making to be glamorous and exciting. It was, to a certain extent, but sitting there listening to the actresses on repeat and reading about the president's ex lamenting over her heartbreak was taking a toll on Clémence. Sophie did tell her it would be grueling, but she didn't realize that meant boring. She was starting to respect actors a little more, for their patience and their skill.

When that scene was finally done, they were able to take a short break as the crew set up for another shot in the café.

More fans had gathered on the street. Many were leaning over on the gate to take pictures, and security did their best to contain them. Sarah convinced Sophie to go greet the fans and take some pictures. Sophie was surprisingly shy, but she agreed. If she was going to be a movie star, she might as well get used to the attention and the fans.

After they signed some autographs and took pictures with their fans, they ducked back into the café. Sophie led Sarah into the very back. Clémence followed, knowing that this was Sophie's way of getting Sarah to talk to her alone.

"Amazing job," Clémence said to the two of them. "You guys did a bazillion takes."

"I could say the same for you," Sarah said.

"Yes. Pretending to drink coffee does require a certain skill," Clémence joked.

"Excuse me, girls. Drinking all that fake wine comes with consequences." Sophie went downstairs to use the restroom.

Clémence was left alone with Sarah. They chit-chatted about the movie industry, and Clémence acted extra interested, since her cover was that she wanted to learn about it for her career change. She told Sarah that she hoped to get into producing films someday. Clémence could, if she wanted to, so it wasn't a complete lie. Since she had the Damour fortune, she did have enough money to invest in a film should she ever want to.

"But right now, you're a baker?" Sarah asked. "How cute."

Clémence couldn't help but find Sarah cute too. She was one of those perky blondes whose smile was infectious.

"It's fun," Clémence said. "But I'm one of those people who have a lot of different interests. It's hard to stay still and stick with one. What about you? Did you always want to be an actress?"

"Always, always." Sarah laughed. "I was one of those little girls who would pretend to give Oscar acceptance speeches into my hairbrush."

Clémence thought about Nicole, about how close she'd been to winning an Oscar. Sarah had never even been nominated. How jealous had Sarah been?

"I'm sure you'll get there," Clémence said.

"There's no rush. Meryl Streep was twenty-eight when she appeared in her first film, and look at her now. She's my role model. I see acting as a lifelong craft to be mastered."

Clémence saw that Sophie had come back from the restroom. Sophie saw them still deep in conversation and started chatting with the makeup girl to give them space.

Clémence pretended to get a text. "It's from my boyfriend," she said. "Aw, he's so sweet. He's just texting to tell me he misses me."

Sarah's eyes lit up. "Who's your boyfriend?"

"His name is Arthur. Here–" She showed her some photos of him on her phone.

"Ohh, he's cute," Sarah said.

Arthur was handsome. With his warm brown eyes, strong cheekbones, and kissable lips, he was quite the catch.

By bonding with Sarah over girly matters, Clémence created the perfect opening to ask about her relationship with Elon.

"What about you? Are you dating anyone?"

Sarah giggled demurely. "Well, there is this guy. He's not in the industry, thank goodness."

"What does he do?"

"He's a businessman. He's a bit older than I am, but he's cute."

"Do you have any pictures?"

Sarah looked hesitant. "We're not public or anything."

"Oh, I won't go to the press. I promise."

"Oh, what the heck. You look like someone I would trust. Here."

She took out her own phone and showed Clémence photos of her and Elon. Elon was a distinguished man in his forties. He had a serious face that looked on the verge of a scowl, but here, with Sarah, he looked at ease. They posed in front of the Louvre, underneath the Eiffel Tower, and at the Pont des Art, putting a love lock on the bridge. Clémence forgot that Sarah was a tourist in Paris and would be as excited as any American to visit the city's most popular tourist attractions.

"Hey," Clémence said slowly. "I know him. Is that Elon Marchese?"

"You know him?" Sarah turned, eyes wide with excitement.

"Well, not personally, but I've seen him at parties."

"Oh, of course. You're friends with Sophie, so you must be part of the fashion set. Of course you would be in the same crowd."

"I'm not that fashionable," Clémence said modestly. "How long have you been dating?"

"About a year." Sarah sighed dreamily. A year into the relationship and she was still in the honeymoon stage; Sarah must really love Elon.

"It's funny. I've read about him in *Hello* magazine once. I thought he was dating Nicole Blake."

Sarah's face darkened a bit. "Oh. Well, it's a long story. They used to date."

"Really?"

She sighed. "I suppose now that Nicole has passed away, I can say it."

"It's a tragedy, isn't it?" Clémence looked at Sarah's face carefully to observe her reaction.

Sarah did look sad. "It is. It's unfortunate that we never got along, although I tried."

"Why didn't you get along?"

"It was the whole thing with Elon. They went out for about eight months before Elon and I started going out. It was all hush-hush. Sarah was so secretive that no one even knew she and Elon were an item. There were speculations, sure, but no real proof. Then he dumped her and started going out with me. We'd met at the MET Gala. The thing was, Elon never cheated on her, but I do admit that maybe we jumped into the relationship too soon after their breakup.

"I personally didn't know they had gone out until I realized how Nicole was being towards me whenever I ran into her at events and parties. All these backhanded compliments at first, then the blatant rudeness. She even threatened me once at the Vanity Fair party, told me she wished I'd die after what I'd done. I told Elon because he was my date, and that's when he told me they used to date. He'd dumped her because she was too demanding, too manipulative."

"So this was why you and Nicole were always rivals?" Clémence asked.

"Yes. From then on, Nicole wanted everything I wanted. She was like a child. She was never able to get over the fact that Elon didn't want her anymore. If she heard I wanted a role, no matter how insignificant, she'd fight tooth and nail to get it. She took my perfume campaign, my magazine covers, everything she could get her hands on. The girl was mean and vengeful, but in the media, she was still a darling. Fake was what she was.

"I almost backed out of this film when I heard that she was going to play my sister, but Elon convinced me to do it. If I backed out, I would be letting her win. I don't care if I don't have a starring role. I just want to work on sets with people I respect, you know? Chris is a great director, and I just want to keep working with talented people. That was one thing Nicole didn't get. She was all about the fame and accolades."

"That sounds like a nightmare," Clémence said. "So Nicole didn't date anyone else throughout this?"

Sarah couldn't help but roll her eyes at the thought. "Oh, of course she did. But it was mainly for her own gain."

"What do you mean?" Clémence asked. "As far as the public was concerned, she was single."

Sarah looked her in the eye. "The movie was about two sisters with equal screen time when I signed on. A few weeks into it, her role was expanded into the starring role, and I was the supporting actress." Sarah tilted her head to Chris Collins. "People might think it, but I'm not naive."

Clémence gasped, looking at Chris as he enthusiastically told the crew what to do. "Nicole was having an affair with Chris?"

Chapter 16

"How do you know?" Clémence asked.

Sarah shrugged. "It's a theory, but I worked with both of them, and I can smell an affair. I don't know if Nicole loved him, but it sure benefited her to have him wrapped around her finger. He's one of the most brilliant directors around, and he was surely going to cast her in other movies after we wrapped this one. I suppose she was angling to be his muse."

"What about his wife?"

"I don't know if she knows, but by the way she's always hanging around on set, she smells something too. She must know her husband's not the kind to remain faithful."

Speaking of the devil, he was walking toward them now. The wide grin was still spread over his face, and he clapped to get their attention. "Girls, we've set up for the next shot. Sarah, I need you and Sophie on the street, walking out of the café and turning the corner."

"It was nice chatting with you," Sarah said to Clémence.

"You too."

Sophie broke free from her conversation with the makeup artist and passed by Clémence before joining Sarah and Chris.

"How did it go?" she whispered to Clémence.

"You'd be relieved to know that Sarah didn't do it. You're right."

"Any idea who did?"

"Maybe. The director's calling you. I'll bring you up to speed when you're done shooting. I still need to do a little investigating to confirm my suspicions."

"Okay," Sophie said. "I'm so glad Sarah's not the one."

Since her services as an extra weren't needed for this scene, Clémence called Inspector Cyril St. Clair.

"*Âllo?*" Inspector Cyril St. Clair barked into the phone.

"So, I'm close to catching Nicole Blake's murderer," she said casually. "You guys better get down here, but dressed like civilians. Track my whereabouts on my phone. By the time you get here, I'll have the killer confirmed."

Cyril begrudgingly grunted in agreement. She knew he was dying of curiosity as to who it was. So was she.

It was either the director or the director's wife. Who had more of a motive?

She took a deep breath and walked out of the café.

Chris was busy blocking the actresses on the streets. Fans were still straining to watch the action from the other side of the gates, and some people were looking out the windows of their buildings down. Clémence spotted Cynthia Collins a few feet behind her husband. The way she was babysitting her husband was desperate and pathetic. She must've been a little crazy. Crazy enough to kill?

Clémence took a deep breath, summoning up the courage to go up to her. She didn't like confrontation, but she had plenty of experience now, which had turned her from a lamb to a lioness. She marched right up to Cynthia.

"We need to talk in private," Clémence said.

At first, Cynthia gave her the death stare, but upon seeing the determination on Clémence's face, she relented.

"What's this all about?"

"I think you know."

Before she could protest, Clémence grabbed her by the wrist and pulled her away. She pulled her inside the café, which was now dim and empty since the cast and crew were all filming outside.

"You know your husband cheated on you, don't you?" Clémence said to her in a loud whisper.

Cynthia's eyes narrowed like those of evil villainesses in movies. "Who are you? And how dare you?"

"Come off it. Why are you following him around, monitoring his every move?"

"He's my husband." She sniffed. "What business is that of yours?"

"He cheated on you, and you're afraid he's going to cheat again."

Cynthia snarled. Her fists tightened. Clémence braced for signs of violence. But to her surprise, Cynthia let out a sob.

"He said he wouldn't do it again," she whimpered. "With that horrible actress."

There were tears forming in her eyes. This cold woman. She was as fragile as the ice over a lake. And she was beginning to crack.

"He was going to leave you," Clémence prompted.

"I was pregnant with my first child, and I caught him in the trailer one day with *her*. I was so distraught I almost lost the child." She was sobbing now. "And I've always been paranoid, which is why

I come on set, to make sure that he doesn't have chemistry with any of the women."

"What did you do to Nicole Blake?" Clémence asked.

"Nicole Blake?" Her eyes widened. "I didn't do anything to her."

"Come off it. She was an affair with your husband."

"What?"

"You knew that."

"I didn't!" Cynthia protested.

"Deep down, you knew that, didn't you?"

"No!"

"She was pregnant with your husband's baby."

"Pregnant?"

"Are you playing dumb?" Clémence was losing her patience. "For a woman as paranoid and astute as you are, you're telling me that you didn't know?"

"No!"

Clémence kept at it. She kept barraging Cynthia with questions until the police came. Cynthia was in a fit of tears, but she answered each one.

Inspector Cyril St. Clair led the way to the back of the café. Three men dressed normally in dress shirts followed him.

"Well, Damour? Who are we arresting?"

Clémence turned to Cynthia, whose eyes widened in fear.

Chapter 17

"You're arresting Chris Collins," Clémence said. "He did it. He killed Nicole Blake."

"Who?" Cyril asked.

"The director of this film," Clémence said with exasperation. "He's out there right now. This is his wife Cynthia. At first I thought it was her, but I just confirmed it was Chris. It was Chris all along. He had the stronger motive."

"Why did he do it?" Cyril asked.

"Bring him here, and we'll get to the bottom of it."

"Are you sure you've got the right man?" Cyril asked. "Don't want to look foolish now."

"Oh, Cyril." Clémence grinned. "Have I ever made you look foolish?"

He scowled.

"If I'm wrong, you don't have to write that letter," Clémence said.

"What letter?"

"You know what I'm talking about."

Cyril stared at her for a couple of seconds, but he relented. "Fine." He waved to his men. "Come on."

"Not that you were going to write it anyway," Clémence muttered under her breath.

A minute later, they came back in with Chris.

"What's this all about?" Chris asked.

Clémence crossed her arms. "Don't play innocent, Chris. It's you."

"Me?" His voice was calm, but his lips had a slight quiver.

"You're the killer. You killed Nicole, then you killed Rachel."

"Why would I kill my star and ruin my own film?"

"Why don't you tell us?" Clémence tilted her head at him. "I'm all ears."

"That's crazy. I've got nothing to gain from it. Her death messed up the entire film's schedule. We had to rewrite the script, and we're over budget."

"Tell us about the affair," Clémence said.

Chris looked between Clémence and Cynthia. "What affair?"

"Your affair with Nicole Blake."

“There was no affair,” he said. “Cynthia. Tell them.”

Tears streamed down Cynthia’s face, but she only turned away.

“Cynthia, honey–”

“She’s said all she had to say to me,” Clémence said. “Now it’s your turn to do the talking. Nicole had a red leather agenda, where she’d written in her meetings. They were coded, but I’ve managed to decipher the codes. Honcho. That’s who she was meeting the night before her body was found. Your wife tells me that it’s your little nickname. What you like to be called in bed. Head honcho.”

“Cynthia!” he protested, but his wife still wouldn’t look at him.

“Nicole showed up for your meeting. You met at the riverbank of the Seine for a little evening stroll, and perhaps a little nightcap in the boat you rented for your stay here in Paris. Your wife told me about that. You take your family around in the Seine during the day, then your mistress for a roll during the night. You were careful, only going out one morning and one evening each week, whenever your schedule permitted it. After you cheat on your wife once, you can’t have a second strike against you, can you? If you got caught again, Cynthia was going to divorce you, and you would lose everything.”

"It's true that I cheated on my wife once," Chris said. "But that was a long time ago. I didn't have an affair with Nicole Blake."

Clémence rolled her eyes. "A cheater and a liar. She told you she was pregnant, didn't she? Wanted you to leave your wife. Nicole loved seeing people squirm, backing people into corners. And you squirmed, alright. A child would ruin you. Not just your family, but your career. You work for Harper Studios. If you lost your wife, you'd lose all the things you've worked hard for: your reputation, your burgeoning career, and the luxurious lifestyle that your wife's family's money and connections have provided you.

"After all those years of making crappy commercials, you're just starting to gain momentum with your features. It was only supposed to be fun, wasn't it, your time with Nicole and God knows who else? You never expected the baby, and you never expected Nicole to rub it in your face, twist your arm so backwards. You knew she checkmated you, so you got angry. She wasn't the director, you were. How dare she pull your strings? So you smacked her unconscious then ducked her head into the Seine, made sure she was dead, and threw her body into the river."

Chris remained silent. Clémence could see Sophie and Sarah poking their heads into the café, trying to figure out what was keeping Chris.

"And Rachel," Clémence continued. "You were in her room, trying to find Nicole's agenda. You'd taken Nicole's purse and destroyed her phone, but you knew about the agenda, and it wasn't in there. So you went into her hotel room and found nothing. The next thing to do was to go into Rachel's room. She was supposed to be out, running an errand for Sarah, but she must've gone back for something she'd forgotten. She surprised you, so you choked her and tried to make it look like she hung herself. Messy business, but why not kill her? You've already killed one person."

"There's no proof of any of this," Chris said.

"Oh, there will be," Clémence said. "Surely you've left DNA in that room. The police found it. Why would you be in Rachel's room otherwise? Little did you know who really had the agenda: me."

Chris let out a loud laugh. "Clémence. When you came into my hotel suite, I thought you were the cutest thing. Poking around, claiming there was a murderer on set. But enough games. This is all ridiculous!"

"Your wife is going to testify," Clémence said. "She confirmed that you made an excuse to go out on the evening of Nicole's death. Your alibi that you were going to a restaurant for a late meeting with a producer doesn't check out."

"Cynthia, please!" Chris begged. "Tell them it's not true."

Cynthia slowly turned to face him. Her green eyes shone as she met his. "It is true. I know it is. I knew I couldn't trust you again. I knew you never loved me, and deep down, I know you're ambitious and ruthless enough to do this."

Chris laughed again, a crazy Joker laugh. "I know you were angry about that time, but to be so vengeful you accuse your husband of murder!"

"I've heard enough," Cyril said. "Arrest him. You better get yourself a good lawyer to get out of this one, Monsieur Collins."

Chapter 18

Clémence had rounded up her best girlfriends for a girl's night out. Berenice, Celine, and Sophie all showed up at Le Schmuck, a gorgeous Baroque-inspired restaurant in the 6th arrondissement. After another crazy week, Clémence needed some downtime with her friends.

Madeleine was the last girl to arrive at the table. She was grinning, holding up her left hand, and trying hard not to squeal too loudly in the restaurant. She'd been waiting for her boyfriend Henri to pop the question for some time now, and he finally did the night before.

"It's been so hard keeping it a secret," Madeleine said, "but I wanted to tell you girls all at once. Only Sophie knows, of course."

She held out her left hand, and the girls all leaned in to admire the ring. The diamond was pink, surrounded by smaller white diamonds.

"It's beautiful!" Celine exclaimed.

"Congratulations," said Berenice. "When's the wedding?"

"Oh, I'm still in shock," Madeleine said. "We haven't talked about dates yet. I don't think it's hit me yet that I'm engaged."

"When she comes back down to earth, I'm sure my sister will transform into a giant bridezilla," Sophie joked.

"I wouldn't put it past me," Madeleine said. "But it'll be at least a year to plan, so be prepared."

"Let me see that ring again," Clémence said.

"Here." Madeleine took off the ring and passed it to her so she could have a closer look under the dim restaurant lighting.

"Remember when we were at the Royal Jewels exhibit at the Grand Palais and you said you wanted a pink diamond just like this one?" Clémence said.

"Well, I wasn't exactly subtle with Henri."

"I'm sure you weren't." Clémence laughed.

"What are we drinking tonight, girls?" Madeleine asked. "Aren't we supposed to be eating dinner?"

Clémence poured her a glass of rosé from the bottle they'd already opened.

"We couldn't wait," Berenice said. "So it's drinks first, dinner, then dessert, then back to drinking."

"Sounds like my kind of night," Madeleine said.

Sophie suddenly shuddered. "I can't believe I've been alone in a room with that man."

"Who?" Celine asked.

"Chris Collins. The murderer. He was a better actor than any of us. It took Clémence to expose his lies."

"I wonder how many years he'll get," Berenice wondered.

"A lifetime, I'll bet," Madeleine said.

"And I can't believe Zach Brant is gay," Celine said. "When his rep made the statement, I wanted to cry. But I guess I wasn't completely surprised." She sighed. "I don't know why I always chase after the wrong guys."

"Maybe you need to stop doing the chasing," Clémence said. "Let the guys come to you."

"I agree," Sophie said. "When you make them work for it, they make more of an effort."

"It's probably true," Celine said. "But that's a lesson I missed as a girl. My mom was the biggest flirt. And she's been divorced twice. She's onto husband number three now, and it's not exactly smooth sailing. I don't want to end up the same way."

"Then just try it," Sophie said. "Resist flirting for a while and see who's really interested in you."

Celine thought about it and nodded defiantly. "You're right. I'm ready for a real relationship. I don't think I've ever even dated a guy for more than three months. I'm going to cool off a bit. Stop dating. Just hang out with you guys, enjoy my girl time and my alone time."

Berenice smiled at her in approval. "That's the spirit."

"Love comes when you're least looking for it," Sophie said.

"And so do psychotic kidnappers," Madeleine joked.

"And murderers," Sophie added. "Hey, Clémence, did Marcus ask you to walk in his show?"

"He did," Clémence replied. "But I can't."

"Why not?"

"I'd be terrible. I can't even walk properly in heels in day-to-day life. I'm sure I'll fall flat on my face. Besides, I had a taste of the spotlight, and I hated it. I don't know how you girls put up with a dozen men chasing after you."

"It's annoying," Sophie said.

"Sure it is." Madeleine rolled her eyes. "You love the attention."

"So do you," Sophie retorted. "You'll be at the show at least, right, Clémence?"

"I will. Even better, Marcus has asked us to make cakes to feature in his show, since his collection is inspired by French desserts. Sebastien and I went into his office yesterday to look at his latest collection, and we've sketched up some cake ideas that would go with his clothes."

"It's going to go down the runway?" Madeleine asked.

"Yup."

"Who's going to hold the cakes?" Sophie asked.

"Models," Clémence said. "But don't worry, they're going to be styrofoam inside."

"Oh good," Sophie said. "Some of these models don't have a lot of muscle mass."

"They probably can't eat the cakes either," Celine said.

"We are making an edible cake," Clémence said, "for the backstage celebration. The models will be tempted to eat at least a little bit."

"Oh, I forgot to tell you guys about the astrology reading that Ben's mom gave me," Berenice said.

"Right," Clémence said. "Spill."

"She said something about one of my planets being in Jupiter, and that Jupiter was the planet of expansion. She was certain I was going to have a lot of kids."

"You? Kids?" Celine laughed. "I thought you hated kids."

"I do. So I was surprised. I guess we'll see."
"Did she say something about whether you'd be married?" Sophie asked.

"No. She didn't mention it, and I didn't ask because it's kind of awkward, since she's Ben's mother."

The waiter came back around. "More rosé?"

"Yes, please." Celine grinned at him. He was cute. Berenice shook her head at her to remind her to back off from flirting. Celine's smile dropped.

"I don't think we've had a toast yet," Clémence said. She raised her glass, and the others did the same. "Congrats to Sophie on her first American movie and to Madeleine on her engagement. And Berenice for her future bundle of rugrats. Oh, and Celine for her dating detox."

"Don't forget about yourself," Berenice said.

"Me?" Clémence frowned. "What about me? You mean for making cakes for Marcus?"

The girls laughed.

"You've forgotten already?" Celine said. "The murder. You solved another murder."

"Oh, yeah," Clémence said sheepishly. "Sure. Let's toast to that."

About Madeleines

The French consider these little shell-shaped sponge cakes to be cookies. Kids will want them during their four p.m. gouter (snack time), and so will adults. They originated from Commercy and Liverdun, the northeastern region of France. They have a literary reputation–Marcel Proust mused over them in The Remembrance of Things Past. As simple of a treat as they appear to be, making madeleines requires care and patience. The outcome is a beautiful and unique cake that's browned and crispy on the outside and soft and spongy on the inside. You do need a non-stick madeleine pan to make them. Twelve-cup madeleine pans are easily available online or in specialty baking stores. They're not as difficult to make as other French desserts, say macarons, and they're the perfect little tea cake.

Recipe #1

Traditional French Madeleines

Makes 24

- 1 stick (4 oz) + 3 tbsp unsalted butter
- 1 cup + 1 tbsp all-purpose flour
- 2/3 cup white sugar
- 2 large eggs
- 1 tsp vanilla
- Pinch of salt
- 1 tbsp lemon juice
- 1 tbsp lemon zest
- Powdered sugar (optional)

Melt the butter in a small saucepan until it bubbles and starts to color. Don't let it burn, so don't let it bubble for too long. Spoon 3 tablespoons of butter into a small bowl and set aside. Let rest of butter cool slightly.

In a medium bowl, whisk one cup of flour together with the sugar and set aside. In another medium bowl, whisk the two eggs with the vanilla, salt, lemon juice, and lemon zest until the eggs are frothy.

Add the egg mix to the flour mix. Use a spatula to stir until just combined. Add the melted butter from the pan and continue to stir. Allow a minute for the butter to blend with the mixture, but don't overmix. Cover the bowl with plastic wrap and leave in the fridge for one hour or up to overnight.

Add remaining one teaspoon of flour to the 3 tablespoons of butter that has been set aside. Stir to combine. Use a pastry brush to brush the interiors of the madeleine-pan shell molds so that they are well coated. (You can also butter the interiors first, dust on some flour, and then tap out the excess.) Place the pans in the freezer for at least one hour.

Preheat the oven to 350°F. Fill each madeleine pan with 1 tablespoon of batter. For this recipe, you need pans of twelve molds, but if you only have one pan, you can bake them a pan at a time. Otherwise, place both pans on a baking sheet for easy handling and place them in the oven. Check after 8 minutes and rotate. Check again 5 minutes later. The madeleines should be browning around the edges and a little puffy in the middle. Use your forefinger and press down the center hump. If they are finished baking, they should spring back at your touch.

After removing them from the oven, let cool for 2 minutes. Use a fork to gently loosen the madeleines from their molds then place the whole pan onto a cooling rack or tea towel. Once cooled, dust lightly with powdered sugar on the shell side. Serve.

If you are storing them, do not dust with sugar until you are ready to serve.

Recipe # 2

Almond Praliné Madeleines

Makes 12

- 3/4 cup all-purpose flour
- 1/3 cup + 3 tbsp sugar
- 2 large eggs, room temperature
- 5 tbsp unsalted butter
- 2 tbsp honey
- 2 tsp vanilla extract
- 1/2 tsp baking powder
- 1/4 cup unblanched almonds
- Pinch of salt

To make the Almond Praliné, line a baking sheet with foil and brush it lightly with oil. Set aside. Combine 3 tablespoons of sugar and 1/4 cup of almonds in a heavy saucepan. Place over medium heat to begin melting the sugar. Occasionally stir with a wooden spoon so the sugar melts and caramelizes evenly. Cook to a light amber color. Scrape the praliné from the pan and spread it about 6mm (1/4 inch) thick onto the foil. Let cool to room temperature for 10 minutes. Break the hard praliné into about 3.5 cm (1.5 inch) pieces, place them in a food processor, and quickly pulse until finely ground.

In a small bowl, sift the flour, baking powder, and salt, and set aside. Whisk the eggs and sugar in another bowl until pale and thick, 2-3 minutes. Add the honey and vanilla and beat well. Use a rubber spatula and fold in the flour mix, as well as the praliné. After they are well incorporated, fold in the butter. Press a piece of plastic against the surface of the batter and refrigerate for at least 3 hours or for up to 2 days to firm up.

Preheat the oven to 200°F. Butter the interior of the madeleine molds. Dust with flour and tap out the excess. Spoon batter in the molds until 3/4 full. Bake for 12 to 14 minutes or until golden and tops spring back when touched. Remove pan from oven and let cool for 2 minutes. Transfer to rack to cool.

Recipe #3

Pumpkin Pecan Madeleines

Makes 12

- 2 large eggs
- 1/3 cup + 1 tbsp flour
- 1/4 cup loosely packed brown sugar + 2 tsp for candying pecans
- 1/4 cup butter + more for toasting pecans and greasing madeleine molds
- 1/4 cup chopped pecans
- 1 tsp baking powder
- 4 tbsp pumpkin puree
- Pinch of salt

Preheat oven to 350°F. Chop pecans. Sift flour and baking powder in a small bowl.

Melt butter in a small pan over medium heat. When frothy, reduce heat as it begins to brown and turn a nutty color. When it is brown, pour it through a fine-mesh strainer to remove any solids, into a bowl. Set the butter aside to cool.

You can use the same frying pan to toast the pecans with a teaspoon of butter. When they are turning golden, toss in about 2 teaspoons of brown sugar. Stir the pecans to coat them well. Remove them from the pan and set them aside to cool.

Use a standing mixer or a handheld electric mixer to beat the two eggs together with a pinch of salt until they are pale yellow and thick. Beat in the 1/4 cup of brown sugar, adding it in large pinches as you continue beating. After all the sugar has been added, continue beating until mixture has more volume and becomes like softly whipped cream.

Sprinkle the flour mix on top and gently fold in with a spatula. Next, fold in the butter and the pumpkin. Make sure they are well incorporated. Then fold in the pecans.

Put 1 tablespoon of batter in each mold. They should be 3/4 full.

Bake for 12 to 15 minutes, turning the pan once halfway to make sure they brown evenly. They will be golden and spring back to the touch when they're ready.

Let them cool for a couple minutes in the molds and then release them onto a cooling rack or tea towel to continue to cool.

Recipe #4

Red Velvet Madeleines

Makes 12

- 2 medium eggs
- 1/2 cup all-purpose flour
- 1/4 cup butter
- 1/3 cup granulated sugar
- 1 1/2 tbsp cocoa powder
- 1 tsp apple cider vinegar
- 1/4 tsp baking powder
- 3/4 tsp vanilla extract
- Pinch of baking soda
- Pinch of salt
- Red food coloring, as desired

Melt the butter and set aside to cool. In a small bowl, mix the flour, cocoa powder, baking powder, baking soda, and salt. Stir to combine and set aside.

In a medium bowl, use an electric mixer to whisk the eggs and sugar until tripled in volume and very thick. When the beaters are lifted, the mixture should drop in a thick ribbon. Add the food coloring and whisk until incorporated.

Sift in the flour mixture in 3 portions, folding gently between additions. Take care not to overmix or stir.

Stir vanilla and cider vinegar into the melted butter. Add the butter mix to the batter in three installments, folding gently after each addition. Don't overmix.

Refrigerate batter for at least half an hour. Preheat oven to 200°F.

Butter the interiors of the madeleine molds. Dust flour and tap the excess flour off. Fill each mold with one tablespoon of batter. Bake for 10 to 12 minutes or until center springs back when touched.

Remove the pan from the oven. Let it cool for a couple of minutes then turn onto a cooling rack to cool completely.

Recipe #5

Raspberry and Rose Madeleines

Makes 12

- 1/2 cup all-purpose flour
- 1/2 tsp baking powder
- 1/4 sugar
- 1/3 freeze-dried raspberries
- 1 extra large egg
- 5 tbsp butter + more for greasing the madeleine pan
- 1 1/2 tbsp milk
- 1 tsp light corn syrup
- 1/4 tsp rose essence
- 1 tsp vanilla extract

Melt butter in a small saucepan over low heat. Skim off the foam on top and let it cool slightly.

In another mixing bowl, stir sugar, syrup, egg, milk, vanilla extract, and rose essence together with a wooden spoon until combined. Then stir in butter.

Gently fold in raspberries and flour mixture until well incorporated. Freeze the batter for 10 to 15 minutes.

Brush the madeleine mold with melted butter then dust on some flour. Tap off the excess. Fill each mold 2/3 full. Bake for 11 to 13 minutes or until golden on the edges.

Remove the madeleines to cool on a wire rack.

Recipe #6

Lemon Madeleines with Lavender Glaze

Makes 12

- 3 large eggs
- 2 egg yolks
- 1 1/3 all-purpose flour
- 1/2 cup coconut oil
- 2/3 cup + 1 tbsp sugar
- 1 tbsp coconut flour
- 2 tbsp lemon juice
- 1 tbsp finely minced lemon zest
- 1 tsp vanilla extract
- 1/2 tsp baking powder
- 1/4 tsp salt

Lavender Glaze:

- 1 1/4 cups powdered sugar
- 1 tbsp dried culinary lavender
- 1/3 cup milk

In bowl, add sugar, vanilla extract, lemon juice, lemon zest, oil, eggs, and egg yolks. Beat on medium speed until thick and smooth, about 3 minutes.

Add remaining ingredients. Mix on medium-low speed until well incorporated and smooth, about 1.5 minutes. Set aside batter for 30 minutes.

Preheat oven to 400°F. Coat madeleine molds with more coconut oil or butter. Put a tablespoon of batter into each mold.

Bake in the center of a preheated oven for 6 to 8 minutes, or until edges start to turn golden. Cakes should spring back when touched. Don't overbake. The cakes will have humped backs, and there might even be a small crack on the hump.

Made the glaze by adding the milk and lavender to a small saucepan and bringing it to a boil. Turn off the heat and let sit for 10 minutes. Strain into a bowl to remove lavender buds. Add the powdered sugar and stir until smooth.

Remove the madeleine pan from the oven. Cool madeleines on a wire rack.

Dip the shell side of the madeleine in glaze and let dry with shell side up.

Recipe #7

Earl Grey Madeleines

Makes 12

- 2 large eggs
- 3/4 cup flour
- 1/3 cup sugar
- 5 tbsp unsalted butter
- 2 tbsp Earl Grey tea leaves
- 2 tbsp honey
- 2 tsp vanilla extract
- 1/2 tsp baking powder
- Grated zest of 1/2 lemon
- Pinch of salt
- Powder sugar for dusting.

Melt the butter in a saucepan and add the tea leaves. Stir and allow tea to infuse with the butter for 15 minutes. Strain leaves from the butter using a strainer lined with cheesecloth.

Combine the flour, baking powder, and salt in a small bowl.

Mix the sugar and lemon zest. Add two eggs and mix until thickened, about 2 to 3 minutes. Add the honey and vanilla extract and whisk for another minute.

Add the dry ingredients to the egg mixture very gently with a spatula. Gently mix in the strained butter. Cover with plastic wrap and chill for three hours.

Preheat oven to 200°F. Butter and flour a madeleine pan. Distribute batter equally between the 12 molds. Bake for 10 to 14 minutes. Check if the tops are firm to the touch.

Remove from molds by tapping the pan. Dust with powdered sugar. Enjoy with a nice cup of tea, Earl Grey or otherwise!

About the Author

Harper Lin lives in Kingston, Ontario with her husband, daughter, and Pomeranian puppy. When she's not reading or writing mysteries, she's in yoga class, hiking, or hanging out with her family and friends. *The Patisserie Mysteries* draws from Harper's own experiences of living in Paris in her twenties. She is currently working on more cozy mysteries.

www.HarperLin.com

CPSIA information can be obtained
at www.ICGtesting.com
Printed in the USA
LVHW04s2012040718
582667LV00002B/158/P